CHRISTMAS SHELTER

Praise for Tammy L. Grace

"I had planned on an early night but couldn't put this book down until I finished it around 3am. Like her other books, this one features fascinating characters with a plot that mimics real life in the best way. My recommendation: it's time to read every book Tammy L Grace has written."
— *Carolyn, review of Beach Haven*

"This book is a clean, simple romance with a background story very similar to the works of Debbie Macomber. If you like Macomber's books you will like this one. A holiday tale filled with dogs, holiday fun, and the joy of giving will warm your heart.
— *Avid Mystery Reader, review of A Season for Hope: A Christmas Novella*

"This book was just as enchanting as the others. Hardships with the love of a special group of friends. I recommend the series as a must read. I loved every exciting moment. A new author for me. She's fabulous."
—*Maggie!, review of Pieces of Home: A Hometown Harbor Novel (Book 4)*

"Tammy is an amazing author, she reminds me of Debbie Macomber… Delightful, heartwarming...just down to earth."
— *Plee, review of A Promise of Home: A Hometown Harbor Novel (Book 3)*

"This was an entertaining and relaxing novel. Tammy Grace has a simple yet compelling way of drawing the reader into the lives of her characters. It was a pleasure to read a story that didn't rely on theatrical tricks, unrealistic events or

steamy sex scenes to fill up the pages. Her characters and plot were strong enough to hold the reader's interest."
—*MrsQ125, review of Finding Home: A Hometown Harbor Novel (Book 1)*

"This is a beautifully written story of loss, grief, forgiveness and healing. I believe anyone could relate to the situations and feelings represented here. This is a read that will stay with you long after you've completed the book."
—*Cassidy Hop, review of Finally Home: A Hometown Harbor Novel (Book 5)*

"Killer Music is a clever and well-crafted whodunit. The vivid and colorful characters shine as the author gradually reveals their hidden secrets—an absorbing page-turning read."
— *Jason Deas, bestselling author of Pushed and Birdsongs*

"I could not put this book down! It was so well written & a suspenseful read! This is definitely a 5-star story! I'm hoping there will be a sequel!"
—*Colleen, review of Killer Music*

"This is the best book yet by this author. The plot was well crafted with an unanticipated ending. I like to try to leap ahead and see if I can accurately guess the outcome. I was able to predict some of the plot but not the actual details which made reading the last several chapters quite engrossing."

—*0001PW, review of Deadly Connection*

Christmas Shelter
By
Tammy L. Grace

CHRISTMAS SHELTER is a work of fiction. Names, characters, places, and incidents either are products of the author's imagination or are used fictitiously. Any resemblance to actual events, locales, entities, or persons, living or dead, is entirely coincidental.

CHRISTMAS SHELTER Copyright © 2022 by Tammy L. Grace

All rights reserved. No part of this book may be reproduced or transmitted in any form or by any means, electronic or mechanical including photocopying, recording, or by any information storage and retrieval system without the written permission of the author, except for the use of brief quotations in a book review. For permissions contact the author directly via electronic mail: tammy@tammylgrace.com

www.tammylgrace.com
Facebook: https://www.facebook.com/tammylgrace.books
Twitter: @TammyLGrace
Instagram: @authortammylgrace
Published in the United States by Lone Mountain Press, Nevada

ISBN (eBook) 978-1-945591-36-5
ISBN (print) 978-1-945591-37-2

FIRST EDITION
Printed in the United States of America

ALSO BY TAMMY L. GRACE

COOPER HARRINGTON DETECTIVE NOVELS

Killer Music

Deadly Connection

Dead Wrong

Cold Killer

HOMETOWN HARBOR SERIES

Hometown Harbor: The Beginning (Prequel Novella)

Finding Home

Home Blooms

A Promise of Home

Pieces of Home

Finally Home

Forever Home

CHRISTMAS STORIES

A Season for Hope: Christmas in Silver Falls Book 1

The Magic of the Season: Christmas in Silver Falls Book 2

Christmas in Snow Valley: A Hometown Christmas Book 1

One Unforgettable Christmas: A Hometown Christmas Book 2

Christmas Wishes: Souls Sisters at Cedar Mountain Lodge

Christmas Surprises: Soul Sisters at Cedar Mountain Lodge

Christmas Shelter: Soul Sisters at Cedar Mountain Lodge

GLASS BEACH COTTAGE SERIES

Beach Haven

Moonlight Beach

Beach Dreams

WRITING AS CASEY WILSON

A Dog's Hope

A Dog's Chance

WISHING TREE SERIES

The Wishing Tree

Wish Again

Overdue Wishes

Remember to subscribe to Tammy's exclusive group of readers for your gift, only available to readers on her mailing list. **Sign up at www.tammylgrace.com. Follow this link to subscribe at https://wp.me/P9umIy-e** and you'll receive the exclusive interview she did with all the canine characters in her Hometown Harbor Series.

Follow Tammy on Facebook by liking her page. You may also follow Tammy on her pages on book retailers or at BookBub by clicking on the follow button.

"Home is a shelter from storms—all sorts of storms"

—William J. Bennett

CHRISTMAS SHELTER

SOUL SISTERS AT CEDAR MOUNTAIN LODGE BOOK 13

TAMMY L. GRACE

CHAPTER 1

Gina fought back tears as she pulled away from the airport in Boise. With only five days before Christmas, she hated feeling so weak and alone. Her parents, along with Luke and Jo, plus little Grace and Ollie, were spending Christmas in California with Gina's sisters and their families.

As much as she would have liked to join them, she'd decided to stay home and mind the dogs, her two, along with Luke's two. Grace and Ollie were so attached to Hank and Finn, they cried when they had to leave them at her house, but Luke and Jo assured them the two goldens would have fun with Otis and Winston, especially since they were all cousins.

She smiled when she remembered Luke's gentle way with the two children, who still struggled with the loss of their family. She admired Jo and Luke for their dedication and the way they worked to make the two children part of both of their extended families. As much as their story broke Gina's heart, Ollie and Grace couldn't ask for a better home or better parents. They also had some very cool aunts and grandparents who loved them dearly.

She swiped the edge of her shirt under her eyes and shook her head. She had shed enough tears when her daughters flew off to Florida last week. They'd be gone until after the new year, spending their vacation with their dad at his new place near the beach. They were so excited while Gina felt like a knife had been slammed into her chest each time they gushed about the pool, the blue waters, and Don's huge new house. She was excited for them but couldn't help but feel like a failure.

She lived in an old house she was slowly remodeling, while running Wags and Whiskers, the small pet supply store she owned. She couldn't compete with Don.

She steered Jo's big SUV to Costco to load up on groceries and all the fixings for Christmas. She argued with herself as the pile in her basket grew. She didn't need all this food, but she knew it wouldn't feel like Christmas without all her traditions, and she longed for the comfort of her mom's ravioli, since she already missed her.

She shook her head and chuckled. Like she needed the two pies she had ordered from Mabel at Rusty's Café. By the time the holidays were over, she would probably gain twenty pounds. She added the last item and steered her cart to the shortest lane, anxious to get home before dark.

Tomorrow was the big pet adoption event, and she needed to be at the store early to set up. All the stores along Main Street were helping and hosting animals and since she owned a pet supply store, she had the largest number of dogs to showcase. The cats and smaller animals like rabbits were easier to place with shopkeepers than dogs, so Gina had stepped up to take on the bulk of the larger dogs.

The merchants in Granite Ridge hoped it would drive some holiday foot traffic, and the local animal shelter wished for lots of forever homes. Gina just wanted to survive the busy day.

A few weeks ago, Jo brought two young women, Morgan and Jillian, to Wags and Whiskers to introduce them to Gina. They were clients at Love Links and were currently staying in the group home the nonprofit charity had opened only a few months ago. They were both eighteen, aged out of the foster care system, and had grown close living together at Love Links.

Jo had a soft spot for so many of the foster kids, but Gina could see these two had touched her sister-in-law's heart. They probably reminded her of her own sisters and how they had become a family.

They both loved animals, especially dogs, and Jo hoped Gina would mentor them and perhaps give them some part-time work at her shop, when she could. With Love Links' main mission to provide foster children who age out of the system a path forward for a stable adult life, Jo wanted to make sure these two were on the right track to get jobs where they could support themselves.

Neither had a strong interest in going to college, but she hoped if they were exposed to some options, an interest in some specialized training might grow. More than anything, Jo was thankful the group home had opened, giving the young adults a safe place to get their feet under them and develop a plan to move forward, whether that be college, trade school, or a job.

Morgan and Jillian were regular volunteers at the animal shelter, full of youthful energy and enthusiasm about the adoption event. They offered to help her tomorrow, which Gina knew from experience, could be wonderful or end up being more work than just doing everything herself. Time would tell.

The more she thought about it, the happier she was that

she had picked up two cases of her favorite wines. This would be a long ten days.

At least Luke and her parents would be back before New Year's Eve. Like usual, Jo and Luke had plans to go to the big party at Cedar Mountain Lodge leaving Ollie and Grace the chance for a sleepover with Luke's parents. Gina was tagging along for the festivities. Thinking of the dress she planned to wear, she promised to limit herself to just one glass of wine each night. She barely fit into it as it was.

As dusk settled over the valley, Gina pulled into her driveway. Her brother loved Christmas and went all out this year. Her eyes were drawn to the windows where wreaths hung on thick red ribbons in each of them. He had even hauled a second Christmas tree upstairs and installed it outside on the small balcony. The glittering of its white lights lifted her spirits.

It, along with the multicolored lights along the roofline of her Victorian-style home made it look like an old-fashioned Christmas card. Luke had come over and hung Christmas lights when he decorated his and Jo's house, and the glow of them warmed Gina's heart.

After all Luke had been through in the military and his choice to retire, it was wonderful to see him with Jo and their unexpected, but perfect family. He had a huge heart and was always there to help her parents, her, or even Maddie, with anything they needed.

She wasn't sure she would have made it through these last few years without him. The divorce had gutted her and having to give up the girls for holidays was beyond heart wrenching. Without him, she would have disappeared in a pool of despair, but he had a way of cheering her up and getting her through the worst of it.

She'd have to put her big girl panties on this year, as she would truly be alone. Well, except for the four fur monsters who were sure to keep her busy and covered in snuggles. She had big plans for streaming some shows she hadn't had time to watch and eating a Suburban full of food, apparently.

As soon as she opened the door, that fresh aroma from her tree gripped her heart. It might not feel like Christmas, but it sure smelled liked it.

It took her forever to haul in all the boxes and get everything put away in the cupboards and refrigerator. Hank, still a youngster, was a little out of sorts and over-excited, but he was getting in the groove and following his pack brother and cousins around the house, learning to be a good houseguest.

Finn, of course, had spent quite a bit of time with Gina and her dogs, but Hank hadn't stayed the entire night with Gina until now. He had a crate, so if he couldn't handle sleeping with the big dogs, she'd make sure he was safe and cozy in his familiar spot.

She fed the pack of hungry pups and then ran next door to check on her neighbor Virginia, who lived alone. Gina had a key to her house and, since Virginia had fallen and broken her hip last month, had taken to checking in on her in the evening. She found Virginia in her recliner, watching television, her walker next to her.

Gina admired the tabletop tree she had picked up at the nursery and decorated for Virginia a few days ago, so she'd have something cheerful when she came home from the rehabilitation center. Gina hooked it up to a timer, so Virginia wouldn't have to fiddle with the lights. It gave her living room a warm glow.

Gina smiled at her. "How are you doing tonight?"

Virginia sighed. "I've been better. I'm just worn out. Could I bother you to heat up some soup for me? I just don't have the strength."

"Sure, no problem. I'll bring you a tray." Gina went through to the kitchen and found the soup she had brought her from Stevie's pub. She ladled it into a bowl and popped it into the microwave. While it heated, she sliced an apple and made Virginia a cup of tea, along with a tall glass of water. She added a dinner roll to the plate, put everything on a tray table next to Virginia's chair, and slid it into position across her lap.

Virginia's eyes twinkled as she smiled. "Oh, dear, thank you so much. I don't know what I'd do without you. It's hard to be alone, especially when you've suffered a setback."

Gina sat with her for a few minutes while she ate, the whole time thinking Virginia needed some help. Her son lived out of state and couldn't get time off his work to stay with her, and Gina knew they couldn't afford much when it came to hiring someone to come to the house. Virginia hated being in an assisted-living facility, even though it was for rehab, so that idea was a non-starter.

Virginia could get by with a few hours of help each day. Someone to make sure she got her meals, and some supervision in the bathroom so she didn't fall again, would make all the difference. The problem was finding anyone available and affordable.

For now, they'd have to get by with Gina checking on her and the twice-a-week visits from the physical therapist, Renee, who always timed her visits around lunchtime and went above and beyond to make sure Virginia got her lunch. Renee even pitched in and did the dishes and laundry when she had time.

Gina suspected Renee used her lunch hour to tack onto the normal appointment time to help Virginia. Granite Ridge may not have all the amenities and services of a big city, but it more than made up for it in the kind and caring community-minded people who lived in the quaint mountain town.

Gina wanted nothing more than to get in her pajamas and snuggle under her quilt, but she stayed until Virginia finished her meal, then did the dishes, and made her another cup of tea before refilling her water glass. Gina made sure Virginia took her medication and helped her to the bathroom before she wished her a good night and hurried back to her own house.

She heated up some chicken fettuccine she had brought home from the store and poured herself a glass of Chardonnay before she settled into her favorite chair. The dogs piled next to her on a large dog bed, and she tuned the television to the show she had been waiting to binge, *Brokenwood Mysteries.* It was set in New Zealand and featured a quirky cast of detectives.

The comfort of the creamy sauce that covered the noodles paired well with the buttery taste of the Chardonnay. The wine soothed her troubled soul and she poured one more glass to enjoy while she watched television.

After finishing her dinner and two episodes, she attached leashes to the dogs' collars and bundled into her warm coat and boots. They'd been cooped up today, and she wanted to give them a chance to stretch their legs before bedtime.

Carrying her flashlight and adding a headlamp, she led her pack around the residential blocks. Thankful she had stuffed plastic bags in every coat pocket, since they all decided to do their business on their walk. At least they chose to do it on the way home, so she didn't have to carry the bags far.

She took in the festive lights throughout the neighborhood, which made the winter night much less dark. She grinned when she returned to her own driveway. Luke had already proclaimed her house the best, and she couldn't disagree. He was a perfectionist, and it showed in the neat installation of the colored lights along her roofline and the wrapped posts on her porch. Not to mention the nets of lights in her shrubs and the twinkling snowflakes that dangled across the top of her porch.

Her eyes couldn't help but draw to the lights of the tree on the second-floor balcony. It made her want to sleep upstairs next to it.

She loved the decorations, and the beauty of it took away some of the sting of missing her family. She hurried up the steps and ushered the dogs through the porch and into her warm house. After everybody got a treat, they settled back down, and she snuggled under her favorite Christmas quilt her mother had made and hit play on the remote.

With all the lights off, except for the glow from the television, the twinkling lights on the huge tree in the corner of her living room comforted Gina. The shimmering ribbons of the gifts under it caught her eye. She had given the girls their presents early, but her family had agreed to open gifts together when they returned from California. She breathed in the fresh scent of the Fraser fir and shut her eyes. It smelled like all the Christmases she remembered.

The tree made her think of Leslie, a classmate of hers who had returned home to Granite Ridge this year to take over the nursery and tree farm that had been in her family for generations. When Gina picked up her trees and the festive wreaths that hung in her windows, Leslie, who had always been outgoing, made her promise to meet up the day after Christmas, *when she'd get her life back*, for dinner.

She and Leslie had hung out in high school but hadn't kept in touch much. It was fun to see her again and with the girls gone, she jumped at the chance to have something to do. She promised to meet her at Cedar Mountain Lodge for a post-holiday visit.

She'd best get used to spending time without the girls over the holidays. Her eldest, Raylynn, would graduate in spring and be in college next year. Her daughter already had her mind made up that she was going to a college in Florida, close to Don. Two years later, Megan would graduate. Now that Don lived in a tropical paradise, Gina didn't hold out much hope the girls would ever choose to spend the holidays in Granite Ridge.

She could have made a big deal about it, but they were old enough to decide where they wanted to go, and she didn't want to force them to stay with her. In all honesty, she probably would have chosen Florida over the typical small-town celebration they had each year.

She burrowed deeper under her quilt. With the chill in the air, she wished she had started a fire, but it was too late. She needed to go to bed soon but couldn't resist another episode. She'd have a fire tomorrow night after her long day at work. She'd need to recuperate all day Sunday and was already dreaming of sitting in front of a roaring fire, snacking on her favorite treats, and enjoying her wine.

CHAPTER 2

Saturday promised to be a busy day. Gina was up early and drove Jo's SUV back to Luke's house and picked up her extended cab pickup. They couldn't fit everyone it in for the airport run, so she had used Jo's that could haul her family and their luggage. With the swap made, she then hurried next door to check on Virginia, made sure she had her breakfast, and was set for the day.

Once home, she found her faithful dogs waiting for her. She let them out in the backyard and the four of them ran in a circle, with her in the middle.

Otis and Watson zoomed by her, as close as they could without touching her. It was a game they loved. She reached out and ran her hands down Watson's back. "Are you boys ready for our big day today?"

The dogs kept whizzing by her, with Finn and Hank stopping for a quick pet as they chased the other dogs. Hank loved the attention and pushed his head into her leg. She bent on her knee and scratched his ears and chin. "You're a sweetie, aren't you? We've got a long day ahead of us, so I hope you're ready for all the excitement. You'll get to meet a bunch of new dogs. What do you think of that?"

With that information, he was off and running again. She let them zip through the yard for a few more minutes and then ushered them to the back porch. Morgan and Jillian were due in less than an hour, and she wanted to have the boys corralled when they got there.

As soon as she arrived at the store, she set up several portable pens and some crates in case any of the potential adoptees needed some alone time. She filled lots of water bowls and made sure they were placed on absorbent mats inside the enclosures. She had plenty of treats and food in stock to handle whatever they needed.

Morgan and Jillian would need to leash and walk the dogs to limit the chance of any accidents, and they were tasked with cleaning up anything that did happen. Gina popped in a pod of dark-roasted coffee and waited as her fancy machine whirred and spat out a steaming cup, before adding her favorite flavored creamer and giving it a quick stir. She inhaled the rich aroma and took her first sip of bliss.

She tossed a few new squeaker toys to her dogs and Finn and Hank, who stuck close to his big brother. She had the four of them in the storage area behind the counter, where Luke had installed a Dutch door. The dogs liked to put their paws on the shelf and watch the activity in the store. Sometimes, Otis and Watson roamed the store, but today was not the day for free-range dogs.

As Gina put the finishing touches on the raffle prize box, Morgan and Jillian came through the door, all smiles. Morgan wore a pretty sapphire-blue hat the same color as her eyes, over her shoulder-length blond hair, while a cheerful red hat covered Jillian's dark hair that matched her deep-brown eyes.

Jo never divulged much about the kids she helped, but

she'd said Morgan and Jillian were both raised by their grandparents, who passed away, leaving them in the care of the foster system. Gina still remembered the emotion in Jo's voice as she shared their story, one that paralleled her sister-in-law's own experience.

The girls had grown up in different areas outside of Boise, but both had been relocated to Granite Ridge right before they turned eighteen, so they'd have the safety net of Love Links.

Jo always told Gina she knew she couldn't help them all, but she was determined to help as many as possible. Gina loved that about Jo—her strength and determination along with her soft heart.

Gina made sure Morgan and Jillian knew where they could fill the water bowls and to secure the gates after they opened them. Gina pointed at the clipboard. "With you two working at the shelter, I'm sure you know all about the applications."

Jillian nodded. "Oh, we've filled out tons of them."

Morgan eyed the forms. "It'll be faster if we help the prospective pet parents, since we know all the questions and can help them think of references. That's usually the section that takes the most time."

The van from the shelter pulled in front of the shop, and Jillian and Morgan hurried outside to help unload the dogs. Eight of them were larger, like her own dogs, and four were a bit smaller. With the girls' help, Gina got the dogs situated in their enclosures and hung their pictures with their biographies on the wire mesh of the enclosures.

The shelter also supplied stacks of cards, like baseball trading cards, with the animal's photo on the front and all the information about the dog and the website for adoption inquiries on the back. Gina placed cards at the counter and around the area where the dogs were on display. She also hung them in the window next to the poster announcing the adoption event.

The applications didn't guarantee an adoption. Prospective pet parents would go through a vetting process, so it was unlikely that many of the dogs would be taken to their forever homes today, and the van would be back to transport them to the shelter at the end of the day.

With only a few minutes before the doors opened, Gina gestured to the coffee machine behind the counter. "How about something hot to drink before the rush?"

Morgan smiled and said, "If you have a hot chocolate, I'll take one."

Jillian was busy retaping one of the dog's cards in the window, but turned to Gina. "I'll take a hot tea, thanks."

While they waited, the girls opened the door to the storage area, while keeping the dogs from bolting through it, and joined them. Otis, Watson, Finn, and Hank were in heaven as the girls gave them belly rubs and let the dogs crawl all over them.

Gina relaxed her shoulders, happy that the girls seemed capable and low maintenance. With it promising to be busy, she didn't have time to babysit them and all the shelter dogs.

Within thirty minutes of opening, and throughout the afternoon, the girls welcomed what seemed like hundreds of prospective pet parents to the shop. In addition to all the interest in the dogs, Gina sold a ton of supplies. She treated the girls to lunch from Fox and Hound, who thankfully delivered their food. Between customers, they nibbled at their meals.

When Mrs. Adkisson came to the door, Gina noticed Morgan rush to it and hold it open for the woman, who was using a walker. Morgan stayed right by her the whole time she was in the store and even helped her convert her walker into a chair so she could sit and hold one of the smaller dogs.

Morgan placed a tiny Chihuahua mix in her lap. "This is Peanut. She's such a tiny girl and a little overwhelmed today."

A huge smile filled Mrs. Adkisson's face. "She's a sweet one. I'm not sure I have the energy for two dogs, but if I did, I'd take her home. It's lovely to see all the interest in adopting them."

"I know. I hope they all find their forever homes today." Morgan let Mrs. Adkisson pet Peanut while she carried her dog food bag to her car for her.

Jillian kept busy helping others fill out adoption applications and reached in to retrieve the smaller dogs for people to hold and pet. She was quick to clean up the spill from one of the bigger dogs knocking over a water bowl. As she placed a bowl of fresh water in the enclosure, she petted the dog's head and whispered, "It's okay. It was just an accident and it could have happened to anyone."

Gina smiled as she watched the natural way Jillian had with the dogs.

When Mrs. Adkisson was ready to go, Morgan helped her up and walked with her to her car.

Gina admired the special softness and patience Morgan had for her older customers.

Morgan greeted everyone that came through the door with a huge smile and engaged them in conversation. "Have you seen these wonderful dogs available for adoption?" she'd ask as she led them to the wire enclosures.

Jillian was kind, but a bit less outgoing with people and more talkative when it came to the dogs. She kept the Christmas tree in the shop filled with ornaments, since it seemed every customer that came through the door, plucked a few off the tree to purchase. They were both kindhearted and hard-working and as Gina watched them, an idea formed. She'd have to call Jo and see what she thought.

In addition to a healthy sales day, the best news was that

several of the large dogs looked like they would be getting their forever homes. Most of the prospective pet parents were anxious to take their dogs home immediately. Gina knew several of them and was happy to write a note of recommendation for them on their applications. Gabby, the manager at the shelter, had told her to do that, as that would help speed up the vetting process. Gina even faxed the applications over to the shelter to help give the applications a head start.

When the shelter van returned to pick up the dogs, Morgan and Jillian helped load the dogs into crates, except for two of the large ones who had already been approved, thanks to the applicants being prior clients of the shelter. Both families came through the door just after the shelter van arrived and were so excited to pick up their dogs.

Each of the families had children and Gina's heart melted as she watched the kids interact with the dogs, who seemed to know they had found their forever homes. The happy dogs wiggled and licked the little faces of the boys and girls and their tails thwacked against their puffy winter coats, eliciting giggles and smiles.

Gina gave each of the dogs a brand-new toy to celebrate and wished them a Merry Christmas as she held the door for them. It made her heart happy to see their tails wagging as they walked down the street with their new families.

They would be having a wonderful Christmas, and Gabby would work hard to get the other applicants approved so they could pick up their dogs next week. Gina's heart ached for the poor pups sitting in the back of the van. She could never volunteer at the shelter, or she'd bring them all home with her. She donated tons of supplies to them but couldn't bear spending time there.

Morgan and Jillian climbed into the back of the van and spoke softly to all of the dogs heading back to the shelter.

Morgan poked her fingers through the slats on Peanut's crate. "It's okay, sweet girl. I think that last lady who held you is going to be your new mom. She's so excited, so don't worry."

Jillian comforted a whining dog. "It's okay. I put a note on your application to rush it through. The man who wants to take you home really loves you and I have a good feeling Gabby will make it happen soon." The more she whispered, the calmer he became.

Gina admired Morgan and Jillian for all the hours they had been volunteering, and it was clear the animals loved them and knew them. The dogs responded to them with quick little licks and lots of wiggles of excitement.

As soon as the van pulled away, she turned off the open sign hanging above her door and blew out a long breath. "What a day." The girls had already cleaned the water bowls and were putting away the enclosures. Gina walked behind the counter and let Finn, Hank, Otis, and Watson out of the storage area. The four of them made a beeline for Morgan and Jillian, eliciting giggles as the girls stopped their work to lavish them with snuggles. Then, the dogs went about their mission of sniffing every inch of the floor where the shelter dogs had spent the day.

The girls made quick work of cleaning up the store and then offered to walk the four dogs up and down Main Street to burn off some of their energy.

"That would be wonderful, thank you. I appreciate all your help today. You did a great job. I'm going to pick up a pizza on the way home, and I'd like to treat you to one. What's your favorite?"

Morgan and Jillian both said, "Hawaiian" and laughed. They waved as they led the dogs outside.

Gina called in the pizza order and hung up the phone, slumping onto the stool behind the counter. She hadn't had time to sit all day, and her feet were killing her. She pictured the fridge full of food at her house and felt guilty for wasting money on a pizza but was too tired to care.

She prepared her deposit and hurried down the street to put it in the night drop box at the bank. She gathered her things and was just turning out the lights when the girls and their four charges came through the door.

"Great timing. Pizzas will be ready in a few minutes, and we can pick them up, and then I'll drop you back home."

Morgan sat in the front passenger seat, and Jillian got in the backseat with all four dogs, who were beyond thrilled to have a human ride with them in their area. Gina pulled up in front of the pizza place and hurried inside, leaving the girls to keep the dogs company.

A few minutes later, she handed Morgan two large pizza boxes and one small one to balance on her lap, while Gina drove over to the group home, decorated with cheerful lights, courtesy of Luke.

Gina helped extricate Jillian from her furry friends in the back seat. "Thank you again for all your hard work today. I couldn't have done it without you."

Morgan surprised her with a sweet hug. "We had a great day. Thanks for lunch and the pizza." Her blue eyes sparkled in the glow of the Christmas lights.

Jillian waved and echoed her thanks while she fiddled with the lights and rearranged a couple of strings that were tucked into the bushes along the walkway.

Gina waited and made sure the girls got inside the house. The dogs crowded to one side of the truck to watch out the window as Gina waved and pulled out of the parking lot.

She stopped by Jo and Luke's house to check on things, leaving the dogs in the car while she checked the mailbox and brought the letters inside, doing a quick walk-through to make sure everything was as it should be.

While she checked upstairs, her cell phone pinged with a message. It was from Morgan. She and Jillian sent a video of themselves holding up the envelopes of cash she had put inside their pizza box. They waved and smiled, thanking her. Gina had tucked a note inside, thanking them for their help and wishing them a Merry Christmas. The video made her smile. The girls deserved a little sprinkling of happiness.

After locking up, she hurried back to the truck and drove the few blocks to her house. She unloaded the dogs and got them inside the house. Dinner was late, and they stood by their bowls, looking at her with questioning eyes.

She put her pizza on the island counter in the kitchen. "I'll be right back. I need to get this to Virginia before it gets any later." She left the dogs looking bewildered at not getting their bowls filled and jogged across the yard.

Virginia was in her chair and happy to see her. "It was a late day at the shop, sorry," said Gina, placing the box on Virginia's tray. "I picked up pizza because I'm too tired to cook."

She made Virginia some fresh tea and filled the water pitcher for her. "How was your day?"

She smiled and nodded as she eyed the pizza. "Not too bad. I've been watching Christmas movies for the most part and napping. This looks so yummy."

"I need to run and take care of the dogs, but I'll be by tomorrow and home all day. I had two young women from Love Links help me at the shop today. They were both sweet and hardworking. I hope you'll think about an idea that came to me today. They both need to find work to support themselves. They're at the group home now, but the whole idea is to get them employed or in school and more independent. I think you could use some help, and Morgan would be wonderful, I think. I know it would be affordable for you."

Virginia looked across the room with quiet contemplation. "I could sure use the help. My son calls all the time but is helpless being so far away. Let me give it some thought and talk to him."

Gina nodded. "I'll call Jo and see what she thinks. I would still be around but would feel better if someone were with you all the time."

Virginia smiled at her. "You're such a sweet one, Gina. I'm so glad you're my neighbor. Let me know what Jo and Luke say."

Gina stood and made her way to the door. "Have a good night, Virginia. I'll talk to you more tomorrow."

Watching Virginia dig into her pizza only made Gina hungrier. She darted across the lawn and back to her porch just as a snowflake fell on her nose. The promised storm had arrived. She found the dogs waiting behind the door, impatient for their food.

She filled their bowls, adding some fresh veggies, along with blueberries to the top of their kibble. As they had been trained, they waited for the command to eat and then proceeded to gobble their dinner.

Gina's pizza was no longer hot, so she slipped it in the oven to warm it up and changed into her warmest pajamas while she waited for it. She started a fire, turned on the television, and poured herself a glass of wine.

The sight of her cell phone prompted her to send a text to Jo. Along with letting her know the two girls did a great job at the adoption event, Gina shared her idea of Morgan possibly helping Virginia and volunteered to make the introductions if Jo thought it would be appropriate.

Minutes later, Jo replied with enthusiasm and lots of exclamation points. She agreed that Morgan had a special way with older people and promised she'd email the manager of the group home to clear the way for Gina to introduce Virginia to Morgan.

Gina glanced at the clock. Virginia turned in early, so she didn't want to call and disturb her. She'd discuss it with her in the morning. She sighed and opened the cupboard to get a plate.

Having someone around all day to help Virginia would ease her mind. Although not related, Gina had a strong sense of responsibility for her neighbor and no time to check on her more than twice a day. Poor Virginia was much frailer since her fall.

With the pizza warmed, she plucked two slices, pulling them high into the air to dislodge the stringy cheese. Her mouth watered as she carried it to the living room and snuggled into her recliner. She took her first bite and moaned.

She glanced at her tree while she chewed it. This was her idea of the start of a perfect weekend. She pushed the button on the remote to start a new episode and devoured her pizza while she watched.

After the first episode, she added logs to the fire. She glanced outside when she retrieved one more piece of pizza, surprised to see the snow already stacking up on the top of the fence. The weatherman had warned Granite Ridge and the higher elevations to be ready for Snowmaggedon, and it looked like he might be right. The snow swirled in the streetlights, and Gina could tell from experience, it was a heavy and wet snow.

She was happy she didn't have anywhere to go tomorrow. She could stay inside and enjoy the pretty lights on her tree, the warmth of the fire, and snuggle with the dogs all day while the snow piled up outside. She loved the quiet and beauty that snow delivered. Maybe she'd finish that new bottle of wine she'd opened.

By the time another episode ended, all four dogs were sacked out, snoozing in front of the fire. Gina made a pot of tea, checked on the snowfall, which was climbing, and she guessed to be at least four inches had accumulated on the ground.

Gina took a sip from her cup and started another episode. Her eyes grew heavy only a few minutes into it. The next thing she knew, she was startled awake by her cell phone ringing.

She reached for it and frowned at the screen, noting it was after eleven o'clock. "Tommy Lane. What could he be calling for this late?" she mumbled as she hit the green button.

"Hey, Gina. I'm so sorry to disturb you so late. I hope you weren't sleeping," he said.

"Don't worry about it. I'm just watching television. What's going on?"

"Well, I'm down at the animal shelter. They've got a busted pipe and water everywhere, along with a power issue. Bottom line, they've got to find a place for the animals for a few days until they get rid of the water, and I'll be waiting on a part for the electrical problem. With this storm, I'm not sure I can count on it being here Monday. I volunteered to call you, and I know it's a huge ask, but they've got six dogs that need a temporary place to stay."

The apprehension in his voice came through with his plea. She looked at the four dogs still sleeping on the living room floor. Six more would make ten dogs. That was crazy, but she couldn't say no.

His deep voice came through the speaker. "If it helps, most of them are smaller; the biggest is a Labradoodle. I'd take them myself, but I live so far out and don't have a fenced yard, with Zap living inside and not much of a wanderer. I'm happy to help with them, too. We just need to get them out of here and somewhere safe. Even the back of your shop would be better than nothing."

She wouldn't put the poor dogs in the storage area.

Tommy was desperate, she could feel it through the phone. "I'm sure we can make something work." She looked down at her pajamas. She'd only had one glass of wine, so driving shouldn't be a problem. "I can be there within thirty minutes."

"Oh, no. I'll bring them to you. I've got them loaded in my work truck already. I can be there in fifteen. Thanks, Gina, you're a real lifesaver."

She disconnected and sighed. "So much for spending a quiet Sunday at home." Ten dogs. What was she thinking?

CHAPTER 3

With a bit of reluctance, Gina left the warmth of her quilt and threw on a heavy cardigan over her pajamas. The thermal shirt could pass for loungewear, but the snowmen and penguins scattered across the pants gave off a definite pajama-vibe. She didn't have time to change.

She went to the back porch to look it over. It was an enclosed space that was used as a catch-all. Part mudroom, part storage, and it housed an extra freezer, plus a smattering of furnishings used more during the summer.

It would probably be the best place for the dogs to bed down for the time being. She was certain they'd come with crates since the shelter used them to transport the animals.

She opened the door from the kitchen wider to let some heat flow out onto the porch. The snow was still falling, and she was glad she didn't have to go out in it.

Florida sounded heavenly right now.

She eyed the space on the porch and stacked and shoved everything to one side, leaving a large, open area in the middle. She remembered she had a wire enclosure she had used long ago. She stuffed her feet in her boots, donned a hat and her jacket, and went out to the unattached garage connected by a breezeway. She hadn't used the portable pen for years, so it took some rummaging, but she finally unearthed it and carried it to the back porch.

She took off the plastic she had wrapped it in and lugged it inside. She stepped back into the living room, warmed her hands by the fire, and added another log to keep it going.

The flash of headlights announced Tommy's arrival. The dogs followed her through the house, inquisitive at the late-night activity. She hurried to the front porch and waved at Tommy, who held two crates as he walked toward her, with Zap, his black Lab at his heels.

"Hey," he said. "Do you have a plan on where to put these guys?"

"I just found an enclosure and was going to set it up on the back porch, provided they can all get along and be together."

"Gabby made sure all of these were good roommates, so I think they'll be okay."

"Okay, great. I just need to get it set up, and we need to warm it up a little bit. I keep it shut off, so it's cold out there. Zap can come in and bunk with my dogs. I'm watching Luke's dogs as well, so there are four of them in the living room."

"I think we're risking you becoming a crazy dog lady with ten dogs, aren't we?" He laughed and set the crates on the porch. A long-haired chihuahua stared out through the wire door. Gina noted the card on the crate with her name, Olive. The other crate held a Yorkie named Pixie, who shook, her big brown eyes filled with worry. They were both so tiny.

Gina welcomed Zap with one of the towels she kept in a

basket on the front porch during winter months. She made sure his paws were free of snow, before ushering him inside. The other four dogs hurried to greet him, their tails in full wag mode.

Gina shut the door behind her, hoping her tree would survive the excitement of the five rambunctious dogs. "I'll get to work on setting up their playpen. Before you come in, could you go out to the garage? I've got a portable heater out there, right next to the door. We can use it to keep things warm on the porch."

Tommy nodded. "Sure, I'll get on it and meet you in the back."

Gina made the four dogs and Zap snuggle together on their beds in the living room while she carried the crates through to the porch. Her fingers were cold, which made clipping the panels together difficult. Minutes later, she heard boots stomping on the back step and looked up to see Tommy holding the portable heater.

She took it from him and plugged it in, smiling when it turned on and heat poured from it.

Tommy grinned. "I'll get the others and be right back." He hurried around the corner of the house.

She continued to work on the panels, and he came around the back of the house and deposited Stubbs, a Corgi, and Gonzo, a scruffy, grey terrier mix. The third crate he set down housed Pudge, a chubby, long-haired Dachshund, who was barking. The last guest, Archie, the Labradoodle arrived on a leash, held by Tommy.

Tommy looked down at Archie, the dogs' eyes buried in the thick curls of his golden-red fur, wagging his tail and wiggling with excitement. Tommy shrugged. "I didn't want to jostle him around in that crate. He's a little too big to carry, and it would appear he's a super fan of snow."

Gina laughed at the snow covering his snout. "He'll fit right in with the crew I have in the house now."

Tommy stomped the snow from his boots and slipped them off, leaving them on the heavy mat just inside the porch door. He handed Gina Archie's leash and got down on the floor, snapping the rest of the panels together, effortlessly.

She reached for another towel from the pile she had brought with her from the front porch and dried Archie's paws, removing the snow that had packed around them. With the pen ready, Gina led Archie into it. "You're such a good boy." She rubbed under his chin, and he leaned his head into her hand.

"I'm going to make one more trip out to the garage. I've got some bins with some samples and stuff from the store and have some dog beds in there, plus some of these dogs could use some sweaters."

"Do you want me to put the rest of the dogs in with Archie or wait?"

"Go ahead and get them out of their crates. We'll see how they do, but they'll be warmer together."

He nodded and opened Pudge's crate. "Will you quit with the barking now?" The dog went quiet when Tommy picked her up and petted her.

Gina chuckled. "I'll be back in a jiffy."

She made her way through the junk she had accumulated in the garage and to the area where she thought the bins were stashed. She moved a few items and finally found the stack of containers she had put in the garage a few years ago, before she had opened the shop and had been reviewing samples and placing orders for supplies.

She maneuvered the bins outside, shut off the lights, and locked the door. It took her two trips to get all the bins to the back porch. She left the dusty bins under the eaves and left her wet boots next to Tommy's. He had hung his heavy work jacket on the coat hooks next to the door and was working in his insulated coveralls and the dark blue beanie he wore on his head. She carted in a variety of dog beds and a bin full of toys and clothes.

Tommy had transferred all the dogs into the enclosure and stacked the crates in the corner. He put the tote of supplies with all the food the shelter had sent with them on top of the stack.

He was in the pen with the dogs, helping them get acclimated. She handed him the beds and a few toys. Each of the shelter dogs came with their own blanket. Gina retrieved them and suggested he put the blankets on the beds and spread the scent.

While he was doing that, she filled two water bowls and put them inside the dog corral. The six of them hurried to the water and slurped it dry. Gina dreaded the idea of getting all the dogs outside in the snow, but she wanted to keep the porch an accident-free zone, if possible.

Tommy extricated himself from the enclosure and stood next to Gina, watching the dogs sniff and investigate the space.

She caught his eye. "You know we're going to have to take them all outside before they go to sleep, right?"

He grinned. "I'm the one that got you into this mess, I'll handle that. I'll warm up a little and take them all out. I can take first shift, so you can get some sleep."

Gina cocked her head and frowned. "What do you mean, first shift?"

"I told you I'd help, unless it's too weird if I stay over."

She shook her head. "Not at all, that's nice of you. Luke's old room is made up with fresh sheets, so you can bunk in there." She gave him a quick tour of the space and made sure fresh towels were in the bathroom. She pointed to the kitchen. "How do you feel about hot chocolate?"

He grinned and wiggled his brows, his sky-blue eyes sparkling. "I never refuse it, especially if you have those little marshmallows."

CHAPTER 4

❄

Tommy made quick work of shoveling Gina's sidewalks in both the back and front of the house. He carved out an area in the backyard to give the dogs a place to relieve themselves, without risking the little ones being lost in a snow bank.

While he was busy outside, Gina checked on the dogs in the living room. They were all passed out, including Zap. She added a couple of logs to the fire, and Otis opened his eye to see what was happening. It wasn't exciting enough to warrant further investigation, and his eye closed. Hank's head popped up, but he also went back to sleep.

She left them snoozing and tiptoed back to the kitchen to finish up the cocoa. She heard Tommy stomping his boots at the back door and poured the chocolatey goodness into a large mug.

When he returned to the kitchen, his cheeks bright red, Gina handed him a steaming cup of cocoa.

He smiled when he saw the top of it covered in tiny marshmallows and a ribbon of chocolate sauce. "Wow, that's fancy." He sat on one of the barstools at the granite island.

She shrugged. "Like my dad always says, if you're going to do something, you might as well do it right."

Tommy chuckled. "Oh, man, that takes me back a few decades. He was always saying stuff like that at the garage. He's a great guy. I'm not sure my brothers and I would have survived without him and your mom."

The dogs on the porch had settled down and were using Archie as a pillow and warming device, all snuggled next to him. The sweet look on his relaxed face assured Gina he didn't mind it one bit.

Tommy looked over the huge kitchen. "You've done a great job on the house. I haven't seen it since it was all put together. It looks fantastic."

Gina beamed. "Full credit goes to Luke. I couldn't have done it without his help."

As they were talking and sipping cocoa, their cell phones beeped with a weather alert.

Tommy gritted his teeth. "It seems we don't have enough snow. Now, a blizzard is forecasted for tomorrow."

Gina frowned. "Oh, joy."

"Blizzards mean power outages. Hopefully, not for long, but we'll need to do what we can to keep things warm. I've got a couple of portable generators that will run a few things, if you need it."

"Oh, that's a good idea. I've got tons of firewood but would like to keep stuff in the fridge cold." She glanced at the back porch and wrinkled her nose. "We'll have to move the dogs into the living room if we lose power. The porch is too cold."

He nodded. "Luke had me install an automatic backup generator at their house, so their pipes should be okay. How about your mom and dad's place?"

"Dad has a generator, but it's not automatic, like Luke's. I should probably run out there in the morning." She gasped.

"Oh, Virginia. I'd bring her over here, but ten dogs would be too much. She'd end up tripping and falling."

"I can set up a generator to help her. I've got a few spares."

"They'll open the community center, like they always do, if it's a prolonged outage, but I don't think she'd want to go there. I'll go over in the morning and see what she thinks."

"Okay, I'll take the dogs for their last outing, and I'd better run by the shop and pick up those generators before the storm gets any worse. I'll tackle setting them up in the morning. We'll hit your dad's place and make sure it's set."

Gina helped him get all the leashes attached and tried to keep the leads from getting tangled, but with six wiggling dogs, it was almost impossible. Tommy set out with his charges, chuckling as he tried to get them all moving in the same direction and out onto the snow-covered grass.

Gina's shoulders sagged. Exhaustion had replaced the adrenaline she had been running on since Tommy called. She needed to rest and wasn't one of those lucky people who could operate on little sleep.

While Tommy was busy with the shelter dogs in the backyard, Gina slipped into her boots and took the five dogs to the front yard. All of them loved snow, so it wasn't easy to get them to focus and stop playing in it. Finally successful, she led them back to the house, where she wiped and dried twenty paws before she got them settled next to the fire.

Tommy was on the porch, attempting to wrangle the six dogs and dry their paws and entire bodies before putting them back inside their corral. She took over, and he left to pick up the generators.

With the heater, the back porch was toasty, and Gina's four-legged guests soon settled down and piled together, again using Archie as their furry headrest. She left them to sleep, hopefully, down for the rest of what was left of the night, actually morning, since it was well after midnight.

She padded back into the living room, added more wood to the fire, and curled into the couch, burrowing under the heavy quilt. Despite trying to stay awake until Tommy returned, sleep tugged at her, and her eyes closed.

※

The aroma of coffee lured Gina from sleep. She opened her eyes, squinting with confusion as she took in the lit Christmas tree and roaring fire. She threw off the quilt, stumbled to the window, and in the dim light of dawn, made out what had to be more than a foot of snow. The pile of dogs she had left on their beds was missing. She walked into the kitchen where she found Tommy at the stove, scrambling some eggs, and the dogs sat at attention, watching him.

"Morning," he said with a grin.

"I can't believe you let me sleep through. We were supposed to trade off." She reached for a cup and poured the freshly brewed coffee into it. "I didn't even hear you come back."

As she passed by him, she noticed his short, sandy hair was still wet from his shower, and the faint scent of citrus tickled her nose. He looked well-rested and was in fresh clothes. She remembered her penguin pajamas and could only imagine her hair sticking out. It was too late to fret about it now.

"Ah, don't worry. I put the generators in your garage and grabbed the bag I always keep at the shop with fresh clothes and stuff in case I get stuck working all night. Everyone was sleeping when I got in, so I just caught a nap in Luke's old room and got up a few times to check on the dogs. They did well all night, and I just got in from taking them out for a quick walk."

He added some shredded cheese to the eggs, buttered two

slices of toast, and put in two more. Gina's eyes widened. "You're pretty handy in the kitchen."

He laughed as he added the cheesy eggs to the plate with toast and handed it to her. "I can do the basics. Lots of years of taking care of my brothers helped train me."

She took the plate. "Thank you. This looks great."

He joined her at the granite counter with his plate and a fresh cup of coffee. "I didn't feed any of the dogs yet, since I wasn't sure how much to give them and didn't want to mess up their routine."

"I'll take care of it when we're done with breakfast." She knew from selling Tommy Zap's dog food what she ate, and it was the same brand she fed her dogs and Luke's, so that would make it easy. "I'll feed our brood first and then feed the others separately. Sometimes dogs can get territorial over food, and we don't need any problems."

He finished his plate and started to wash it. She waved him away. "Just leave that. You've done plenty. I'll clean up and get everyone fed. You can get started on the generator. Then, I'll run over to Virginia's and talk to her."

He nodded. "Sounds good. Once we're done here, I can head out to your dad's place and make sure things are set. According to the forecast, the blizzard is supposed to hit around noon."

She dug in her handbag and gave him a keyring. "Here are the keys to the house and Dad's shop. He's been talking about having you add that auto-switch but hasn't gotten around to it." She rifled in her junk drawer and added a key on a golden retriever chain. "This is to the house, so you have it while you're staying here."

He nodded and tucked it into his pocket. "I remember helping your dad install his system, and we talked about the switch. I'll get it running and turn on a trickle of water, just in case."

He stepped into his thick coveralls, added his jacket, hat, and gloves, and set out the back door.

Gina scurried around like a mad woman, got the five dogs fed, and then relegated them to the living room while she organized food for their guests. The shelter had included a list with the amounts and types of food each of the dogs needed, and she went about filling bowls and lifting the little ones out to feed them.

Archie was the last to eat, and he was drooling on the floor by the time she opened the gate to let him eat his breakfast. It didn't take long for him to scarf down the kibble. She always added some fresh food to her dogs' meals but resisted doing that with the shelter dogs. The last thing she needed was tummy troubles and with the evacuation, they were likely enduring enough turmoil and change.

She got everyone back in the enclosure and hurried to her bathroom. With the chance of a looming power outage, she jumped in the shower and washed her hair. After changing into actual clothes, she sat by the fire for a few minutes, hoping to dry her thick hair.

Using her fingers to separate strands of hair and help speed the process, she deemed her hair dry enough and added one of her favorite winter hats to keep her damp head warm. She opted to leash up Archie and introduced him to the five dogs in the living room, where they jumped from their beds to greet him.

Archie was similar in size and so excited to meet the others. She walked the group into the front yard. Her sidewalk was cleared, thanks to Tommy, but all the surrounding sidewalks were stacked with snow, and she didn't have the time or patience to trudge through it with six big dogs.

Her dogs were confused when she turned them back from their usual route down the street and climbed the porch for towel drying. Once she got them situated by the fire and added another log to it, she went to the back porch. She left Archie with the other big dogs, where he had piled onto the beds, making himself at home. His pink tongue stuck out of his mouth, and she could swear he was smiling at her.

She led the small dogs to the area Tommy had cleared and urged them to do their business. It took longer than she hoped, but they finished, and she led them down the sidewalk to where Tommy was working at the electrical panel, which was on the side of the house connected to the breezeway.

"How's it going?" she asked.

He turned his head and grinned. "About got it whipped."

"Great, I'll get the dogs back into the house and then head over to Virginia's to check on her and see what she wants to do."

After several minutes of drying all their paws and bodies, she got them inside their enclosure and made sure their water bowls were full. Pudge whined, and then Pixie chimed in with a few barks.

Gina went into the living room and retrieved Archie. They probably missed him, or at least she hoped he could stem the unrest. Once Archie was with them, he settled down on the floor, and the others snuggled in next to him, quiet as church mice.

Gina took advantage of the calm and hurried next door, through the snow that almost reached her knees.

She let herself in with her key and called out to Virginia, hoping she wouldn't startle her. She found her in the recliner in the living room.

Gina brewed her a pot of tea and fixed her an English muffin with some of Virginia's homemade strawberry jam. Gina carried the plate to the living room and placed it on Virginia's tray, along with a fresh glass of water.

As Virginia ate, Gina brought up the blizzard and the chance of a power outage. "Tommy is over at my place hooking up a generator. I'd just ask you to stay with me, but I've got a houseful of dogs from the shelter I took in. They had a water pipe break and an electrical problem. So, with Luke's, I've got ten dogs."

Virginia's eyes widened. "Oh, my. Yes, I don't think that would be a good idea, not with my walker. I'm still not stable. I'd much rather stay here than go to the community center. I like being in my own place."

Gina nodded. "I figured you'd say that." She explained that Jo had agreed that Morgan would make an excellent caregiver. "She and the other young woman, Jillian, are both kind. I don't know how you feel about having them stay with you, but I was thinking about it last night and thought that might be a good solution. You could give them room and board and maybe a small salary for staying here and helping you. They could do your housework, errands, meal prep, and make sure you were safe."

"My son liked the idea of having someone in the house." Virginia held her teacup, her eyes focused on the mantel. "This is the kind of weather that's perfect for a fire, but I can't even manage tending to that. I hate being so helpless and dependent, but I think what you propose makes sense. I can't afford much, but like you suggested, with room and board, they wouldn't need much."

"I know Jo wouldn't vouch for them if they weren't reliable and trustworthy. They just need a bit of help and direction. Maybe we can talk Morgan into enrolling in the community college program for nursing. She seems like a natural to me."

Virginia was a retired teacher, and her eyes brightened at the idea. "Oh, yes, I can help the girls explore some options for education or work. Actually, I'd like the company, and Lord knows I need the help."

"I'll get in touch with them and see if they can get over here today. With the storm coming, it would be a good idea for them to be here with you. They can tend the fire. Do you need any food?"

She shook her head. "I'm stocked up. Just got a delivery the day before yesterday, so I should be fine and have plenty to feed the three of us. I've been getting the meal delivery from the senior center for lunch, and you've been so good about bringing me dinner. I'm a bit spoiled."

They chatted for a few more minutes, and then Gina stood. "I'll have Tommy come over and hook up a generator to keep your heat on and your refrigerator going. I'll bring the girls over as soon as I can arrange it. We only have a few hours before the storm is due."

"There are two empty bedrooms upstairs, so they're more than welcome to them. They'll need a good dusting and freshening, but they're outfitted and ready. Thank you for thinking of me, Gina. I don't know what I'd do without you."

Gina cleared Virginia's dishes and set out for her house. She was already exhausted, and it was only eight o'clock.

CHAPTER 5

While she left Tommy to take care of hooking up Virginia's generator, Gina put in a call to Morgan. The young woman's cheerful voice came through the phone.

Gina explained she wanted to see if she and Jillian might be interested in staying with her neighbor and helping her with tasks and personal care. She made sure to mention she had discussed it with Jo, who liked the idea. Gina offered to pick them up from the group home and drive them over to meet Virginia and decide.

"Maybe even a trial period for a few days to see how the three of you do. She could use some help and with this storm, I'm worried about her."

Morgan wanted to check with Jillian, and Gina heard their muffled voices in the background. Moments later, Morgan said, "Yes, we'd be happy to meet your neighbor and if we all get along, the idea of staying there and helping her sounds great."

"I think it makes sense to try it out for a few days before you commit. I'll talk to the manager at the group home and make sure that works for her. She can get in touch with Jo if she has any questions."

Gina promised to be there soon to pick them up and reminded them to bring their things. She disconnected and texted Jo, so she'd know what was going on and smooth the way with the manager.

She checked on the dogs, who were resting and quiet. With the thought of losing power, she opened the refrigerator and toyed with the idea of cooking some things before the storm hit. From what Tommy explained, the generator would only support a few circuits, and the oven and microwave took too much power.

They could always use the outdoor grill to heat things up, if necessary. She gathered the ingredients for brownies and the easiest cookies she baked during the holidays. Once she got the brownies in the oven, she tackled rolling the cookie dough into balls and putting the chocolate candy in the middle to make the blossoms she had loved since childhood.

Tommy returned to the back porch while she slid the cookies into the oven. He poked his head through the doorway, confining his wet boots to the porch.

"Whoa, you've been busy. It smells so good."

"I figure we might need some comfort food if this blizzard materializes and keeps us confined to the house."

"I've got Virginia's generator set and was going to head out to your dad's place."

Gina nodded as she stirred. "That's great. I'm going to pick up two of the girls from the group home and take them to Virginia's. She needs some help and has agreed to the idea, at least for a trial. That way she'll have someone there, which will make me feel better. If you run into trouble at Dad's, just give me a call, and I'll run out there."

"Will do. It should be straightforward. I'm going to swing by my place on the way back. Do you need anything else?"

"I don't think so. I've got a ton of food and firewood, so I think we're covered."

He waved goodbye and stopped to pet all the dogs on the porch before he left through the back door. Gina made sure it was locked behind him.

During big storms, power sometimes went out throughout the city, which meant water could be another issue. Gina had some bottled water stored but gathered up containers and filled them to make sure they would have some in reserve. Then she filled the upstairs bathtub and dragged the tree from the center of the balcony to the corner to protect it from the worst of the winds. Once downstairs, she filled her bathtub with water, so they'd have an extra supply of water for the dogs and washing dishes.

She wrestled her best ice chest from the shelf on the back porch and added the frozen gel packs that would last for several days to it. Then, she searched the refrigerator and added the things they would be using most. She wanted to keep the refrigerator and freezer door shut as much as possible.

Once she had it filled with sandwich fixings, meat they could grill, cheese, milk, cream, fruit, and the assortment of pumpkin, chunks of sweet potato, and blueberries she liked to add to the dogs' kibble, she added more gel packs and shut the lid.

By the time she got all that done, it was time to put the last batch of cookies in the oven.

She waited until the cookies finished and then took the dogs, in two separate groups, outside. It was getting colder by the minute, and the wind was picking up speed, making trips outside more undesirable for everyone, even the dogs.

They made quick work of their mission and once Gina had them dried, which the big dogs thought was a great opportunity for a wrestling match with her, she checked her phone and saw a text from her sister-in-law. Jo had talked with the manager and arranged everything so the girls could have a trial period until the first of the year, meaning they'd retain their place at the group home should it not work out with Virginia.

Gina smiled at the great news. She didn't want to be the person who set them on a path that would take their security of the group home from them, but Jo assured her they had to leave the nest, and the group home was a short-term solution, so the sooner, the better, provided they were in a stable situation. Love Links would still help them if they needed it. Their mission was to see young adults who had been foster children succeed, and they would do everything they could to make that happen.

Gina stoked the fire and went to the porch to check on the dogs once more. Gonzo captured her attention first. She reached down and ruffled the top of his head. "You're a sweet one, aren't you?" He relished the attention, moving his head into her hand as if to suggest she continue the petting.

Archie was easy to love, with his sweet eyes buried in the curly fur. His tail wagged as she stroked his ears. "Are you in charge of this group?"

Pixie chimed in with a high-pitched bark and Archie looked at her and then met Gina's eyes. "I know, boy. You're not in charge of her, right?" Gina laughed and made sure to give all of them a pet or a scratch before she wandered back to the living room.

Otis and Watson looked at her with their expressive eyes. They knew she was leaving and were used to going with her whenever she left the house. "I know you want to go, but I need you guys to stay here and watch over everybody. I have to pick up the girls and will be quick about it. Okay?" She bent and kissed both of them on the top of their heads and then did the same to Finn and Hank. Finn's tale thumped against the floor and he raised his paw.

"You are too cute," she said, giving him another quick pet. "You be good and I'll be right back."

She braced herself for the cold as she drove over to pick up Morgan and Jillian. They were excited and waiting for her in the lobby, having already talked with the manager.

Gina helped load their things into the truck and slid behind the wheel, shivering. She stopped by Wags and Whiskers, left the girls in the truck with the heater running, and put a sign in the window saying she was closed until after the storm, adding her cell number for anyone who had an emergency need. Then, she went in the back and turned on the faucet on the utility sink, adjusted it to trickle, hoping it would be enough to keep the pipes from freezing. She didn't own the building, but she didn't need the hassle of the problems that came with a broken pipe.

She had a small freezer with glass doors in the front of the store, with some fresh food products. She carried what was in it and consolidated it into the larger storage freezer in the backroom. With a solid door, she figured it would have a better chance of keeping things frozen if the power outage lasted longer than a few hours.

She grabbed two of the pet gates she used in the store and hurried back to the front door, locking it shut. That was all she could do. The stores on both sides of her were closed, and Main Street was almost deserted.

She drove back to her neighborhood and let the girls out, along with their belongings, before parking her truck inside the garage.

Gina helped them carry their things through the snowy sidewalk to Virginia's front door. She knocked and hollered out a greeting before letting herself in with the spare key.

She found Virginia in her usual spot, relaxing in her

recliner. Gina motioned for the girls to leave their things in the entry area and come into the living room. They both smiled and extended their hands in greeting Virginia.

"You both have such beautiful smiles," she said, holding their hands in hers. "Gina tells me you've agreed to a trial period to see if this arrangement works for all of us. I'm glad you're here."

"Yes, ma'am," said Morgan. "We can help you with whatever you need."

Virginia smiled. "I'll let Gina give you the grand tour, since my mobility is a bit limited. You two can have the run of the upstairs. First thing, we'll need more wood brought in, and the fire started. With the storm coming, we won't want to be venturing outside much."

Gina helped them carry their suitcases and bags upstairs. Their eyes widened at the large bathroom and bedrooms equipped with queen-sized beds. They were used to sharing a room with two twin beds, much like a dormitory.

Jillian chose the room done with green accents and Morgan took the blue one. Gina pointed out a linen closet with cleaning supplies and a vacuum. "You'll need to do some housekeeping up here, dust and whatnot. Virginia hasn't used the upstairs in quite a few months."

Gina led the way back downstairs and showed them the kitchen, making sure they knew how to use the stove and encouraged them to open the cupboards so they could see where things were kept. "Before you take your coats off, let's go out in the backyard, and I'll show you the woodpile. You can move some of it inside to Virginia's back porch to keep a supply dry and handy."

She showed them how to stack it and then led them into the living room, where she demonstrated how to start a fire, crumpling newspaper and adding dry kindling from the container Virginia kept on her back porch. Once the kindling caught, she added a log to the glowing embers and then had Morgan add one, so she'd get some practice.

"Just be sure and keep it going, so you have the extra heat. If we lose power for an extended period, Tommy will come over and start the generator, which will protect the fridge and freezer and run the furnace."

The wind whistled outside, and Gina turned to look out the window. Snow was flying. "I need to get back home. Call me if you need me or come over if cell service goes out. You might want to make something warm for lunch while you have power and fill some containers with water."

The girls nodded while Virginia waved at Gina. "We'll be fine. You get home before it gets any worse."

Gina said her goodbyes and dashed outside and into the swirling snow. She wanted to take the dogs outside again before it got much worse. That was easier said than done, but she finally got it accomplished. An hour later, she had all the dogs dried and huddled together on fluffy beds and blankets.

After adding another log to the fire, she brewed a cup of tea. She put together a pot of soup and left it to simmer on the stovetop for a hearty lunch. They could always reheat it over the fire or on the outdoor grill if they had to. While she was planning, she boiled a kettle of water and poured it into the fancy insulated air pot her mom had given her last year. It wouldn't last all night but would keep the water warm for tea for several hours.

With all her chores done, she grabbed two of the fresh cookies she had baked to enjoy with another steaming mug of tea and had just sat down in her chair, when Tommy hollered out a hello from the back door.

Minutes later, he and Zap came into the living room, where the black dog hurried to join her friends on their dog beds. He followed, balancing a mug of tea, with the plate of cookies and brownies he carried, and took a seat in the recliner closest to the dogs.

"I think we're as ready as we can be at this point. Your dad's place is up and running, I grabbed more clothes and checked on my house, and Virginia is all set."

Gina noticed his cheeks were still red from the frigid outdoors. "Thank you for doing all of that. I'm exhausted, and it's only noon."

"Nothing like a prediction of Snowmaggedon to motivate us, right?" He chuckled as he popped a cookie into his mouth. All the work and running around preparing didn't faze him in the least. Gina envied his laid-back ease.

He took a sip from his mug. "They're still saying we're in for a storm of the century, so I think you're stuck with me for a day or two. At least until we can dig out and if we lose power, it's restored."

She smiled. "You're more than welcome. It's been… nice having someone around." She cradled the warm cup in her hands. "I've been dreading Christmas this year, worried about being alone. A tiny bit jealous that everyone went to California, and my girls are in Florida with their dad."

"I'm sorry they're so far away." He offered the plate of goodies to her before taking a brownie. "These are so good. I'm going to end up eating all of them. I have a weakness for chocolate."

He pointed to the pile of dogs. "Well, you certainly aren't alone." He grinned, and his eyes held a mischievous twinkle. "I'm sorry about saddling you with all the shelter dogs, but like you, it's been nice to have someone to talk to." He glanced at his dog's sweet face. "Other than Zap, of course."

"Right. I'm never alone. Not with all my furry kids here. Did you have plans for Christmas?"

He shrugged. "Not really. I usually work the holidays and let my guys have the time off with their families. Sometimes I go over to my brother's, but not with this weather. The last few years, we've gathered at Paul's. Davey, his youngest son, has Down's Syndrome, and he loves Christmas. It's more fun with kids around, and Davey likes to be at his own house, so I usually make it up there for the day. Not this year though. We'll be swamped with service calls once the storm's over, so I'm going to look at the good side of this forced downtime and relax."

Gina noticed his eyes brightened and his voice softened when he mentioned his nephew. "Paul's in McCall still, right? That's not too far, if the weather cooperates."

Tommy nodded. "Right, and Mike's down in Boise, which is also doable when it's dry. Sometimes we all end up at one house or the other, but with the storm, they opted to stay at their own places. With Paul's plumbing business, he'll be inundated with work after a storm like this one. Mike has been busy all year at his auto repair shop. Usually, business slows down around the holidays, but he's been working on the weekends just to stay on top of things. He likes to close the week after Christmas, but I'm not sure this year."

Gina nibbled at her cookie. "You three brothers are all so talented. Between the three of you, you can fix anything, and you all have successful businesses. You should be proud."

He leaned back in the chair and stared at the fire. "It's always been about survival for us. We learned to fix things because we had to and then later when Mike and I were working for your dad, he helped us refine our skills. He let us tinker and explore, and we figured out what we were good at and liked to do, and then Ray helped connect us with people in the community where we could get a job and learn the ropes."

"Dad's a good guy, and I'm not saying you didn't have help, but you should be proud of what you've achieved. Much of what you three accomplished is a testament to your hard work and perseverance. Making a home for your brothers couldn't have been easy."

He shrugged. "I didn't have much of a choice. Like I said, survival was our goal."

In the pit of her stomach, Gina felt a stab of shame. She had been whining about spending Christmas alone. She'd had a wonderful childhood with loving parents, who provided for their children's every need. They still were there for any of them whenever they needed a hand or advice. They had been a big help when she came back to Granite Ridge after her divorce. Dad had insisted on helping her start her own business and told her he believed in her. He and Mom had worked alongside Luke to help her get everything done.

Tommy and his brothers had been left to struggle on their own after their mother walked out on them. Tommy, the eldest, had been a freshman in high school, the same age as Gina, and had taken on the role of being the head of their household. Gina, along with everyone else, had no idea at the time. The boys had done a good job of covering for their mother and lived on their own in a dump of a trailer.

Her mom and dad knew the family was struggling but had no idea their mother had abandoned them. Had her parents known they were alone, Gina knew they would have taken the boys in, but Tommy made the decision to keep it a secret. More than anything, the three brothers didn't want to be separated and go into foster care.

While Gina had worried about what to wear and who would accompany her to the movies on the weekend, Tommy had scrambled to provide food and shelter for his brothers. Now, more than twenty-five years later, he was still the same. A humble, hardworking, and responsible guy, going above and beyond to help everyone, like the animal shelter and his neighbors.

Without his generosity, Jo said they would have never gotten the group home done. Along with Tommy's sizable donation, he and his brothers had pitched in and done much of the manual labor.

He stood and wandered into the kitchen. "This soup smells great."

"We should probably have a bowl while it's hot and we still have a functioning kitchen." Gina rose and joined him, where he gave the pot a gentle stir.

"I've got some bread to go with it," she said, reaching for bowls from the cupboard.

"Sounds perfect." He made his way to the porch and bent down, whispering to the dogs and picking up the smaller ones to pet them and hold them against his chest.

Gina smiled. He was still the caretaker he had always been.

He had a soft spot for the vulnerable.

Jo was right. He was a good guy.

CHAPTER 6

They had finished the lunch dishes, boiled fresh water for the air pot, and brought the dogs in from another trip outside, when the power blinked off. The house grew quiet, enhancing the whistling of the wind. The gusts had picked up, and the storm was howling down the mountain, blanketing Granite Ridge in an even deeper snow.

Tommy still had his boots on and volunteered to go over to check on Virginia. The portable generator would only run about ten hours on the fuel in it, so he wanted to make sure the girls understood he'd be back over to start it up later in the evening, if the power was still out. He has some spare fuel for both Gina and Virginia, but not an unlimited supply.

While he was gone, Gina lit several candles, taking care to place them in high areas, away from anywhere the dogs might access them. She put a flashlight in the bathroom and on each porch before stoking the fire. While she warmed her hands, she surveyed the living room, contemplating how to move the six shelter dogs into the space.

By the time Tommy returned, Gina had a plan and put it

into action. With his help, they moved her living room furniture to make room for the addition of the dog pen. Once the furniture was situated, she went upstairs and returned with a pile of bathroom rugs and sheets. She placed the rugs down first, working to protect the wooden floors she and Luke had worked so hard to install. She added an old blanket over the rugs and then a sheet.

Tommy helped her install the wire enclosure around the perimeter, taking care to make sure the tiny rubber feet were placed correctly to protect the floor. Gina stood back, hands on her hips, and looked over the pen. She glanced at the big dogs and saw the wide-eyed look of Otis and Winston and laughed.

"I suspect my dogs think they're going to jail from the look they're giving me." She pointed at Zap. "She's the only one that looks relaxed about it. Probably because she's never had to be in a playpen, right?"

He grinned. "She's pretty spoiled, that's for sure. I've let her sleep with me since she was little. A mistake, I know, but I just couldn't help it."

Gina lowered her voice. "Don't tell anyone, but when the girls are gone, these two guys sleep in my bed."

He smiled. "Your secret's safe with me." He wiggled the panels to make sure they were connected.

Satisfied with the sturdiness and comfort of the enclosure, Gina and Tommy began the task of uncrating the dogs. Pudge barked, and Pixie had decided to make it a duet of whining. The high pitch made Gina cringe. She hurried to get them out of the crates.

Once they were all inside the pen, they wandered around, sniffing at the new bedding and giving it a once over. After a thorough inspection, they turned their attention to the big dogs a few feet away from the enclosure.

Moments later, the two headliners of the crazy dog show,

Pudge and Pixie, barked. They fed off each other and if one started acting up, the other joined in the chaos. Olive liked to add in a bark or two, but the main culprits, now, were Pudge and Pixie.

Gina sighed and rolled her eyes.

Finn and Otis looked at the barking dogs and then stared at Gina, as if pleading with her to save them from the tiny demon dogs. Zap kept tilting her head, as if trying to comprehend what the high-pitched barks meant. Hank hid behind Finn, and Watson looked like he was ready to bolt.

Tommy stretched out on the floor next to the pen. The big dogs immediately stepped forward and huddled against him, while he faced the guests, staring at him behind the wire mesh.

With Archie's tail wagging, he kept looking at the big dogs he had met earlier and wiggling. He clearly wanted to join them and play together. Tommy stuck his fingers in the squares and talked to the dogs, almost whispering, trying to calm them.

He distracted them for a few minutes, but then the excitement wore off, and they went back to their barking chorus. Gina shook her head. "We might have to rethink this if they don't calm down."

The relentless barking was unsettling to the other dogs. Gina disappeared through the kitchen and returned with the gates she had borrowed from the store. She put one across the opening to the kitchen and one across the stairs. She rustled up another gate she had stowed away on the back porch and used it across the hallway opening.

"Well, that will confine them to this one room, should anybody decide to attempt an escape."

Tommy opened the enclosure and let Archie out, who went over to the pile of dogs and promptly squeezed into the middle of them. He let him settle in for a few minutes.

Next, Tommy lifted out Stubbs and Gonzo. "I hate to reward the ones making all the noise, so I'm leaving them in there to see what happens. Maybe they'll quiet down."

Gina watched as the Corgi moved toward the big dogs, a bit of trepidation in his steps. All the dogs sniffed at him, while he inspected them, his tiny tail frantically wagging as he greeted the others. Stubbs was a beautiful sable and white color and had the sweetest face, with irresistible eyes.

She looked at the three remaining dogs, all of them yapping. Gina couldn't take it. She picked up the two smallest, Pixie and Olive, and set them near Archie. Hank took an immediate interest in the two of them but kept a safe distance, unsure if their barks would be accompanied by violence. Instead of a bark, a low growl came from Pixie, and Hank backed away, hiding behind Finn.

Gina looked at the Yorkie and with a firm voice, said, "No, Pixie." She shook her head at the dog and glanced at Tommy. "I've never had little dogs, and now I remember why. I can't stand the yipping."

"I've only had one other dog, and he was also a Labrador, so I don't have much experience. Maybe they're just nervous."

He lifted out the last one, Pudge. She waddled near the two barkers, adding a howl for good measure, and settled in close to Archie.

Pixie and Olive ventured away from the pile, and Gina made a sound like an angry cat, herding them back to the others. "I don't need them running all over. Maybe we should try to use the enclosure as a blockade fence around them."

Tommy unhooked a panel and stretched out the wire across the area, bending it around to meet the wall. "That should work. If they get unruly, we'll just have to put them in a timeout in their crates, I guess."

Gina nodded. "Sounds good to me. I've never had to deal

with this many dogs at once, so we'll have to figure it out as we go."

She took another rubber-backed rug, put it inside the fence, and then added the water bowls on top of it. "Hopefully, my floors will survive this."

She and Tommy sat on the floor with the dogs, hoping to help settle them and reassure them. Despite their chutzpah, Pixie and Olive shook, which confirmed Tommy's thought that their aggression came from fear. Gina held them on her lap and after thirty minutes of petting, they calmed.

Gonzo had taken a liking to Tommy and was snuggled close to him, while Tommy petted his ears. Tommy whispered to Gina, "I like his scruffy look."

She nodded. "It makes him even cuter, and he's got a great disposition. Seems easy-going." She pointed at her lap. "These girls need to find owners looking for lap dogs."

Stubbs walked next to Gina and brushed against her leg on his way to the bigger dogs, and Pixie nipped at him. The little dog didn't try too hard and didn't get him but was obviously territorial.

Gina scolded her again and petted her. What she lacked in weight, she made up for in bravado.

Gina moved both dogs from her lap and placed them on one of the smaller dog beds, away from the others. She made a trip to her bedroom and returned with a rechargeable radio. She grinned at Tommy. "Music sometimes works to calm and comfort puppies, so maybe it will work with our guests."

She tried tuning the radio but had no luck finding a station that was broadcasting anything but static. Reception in town was iffy at best, and the storm didn't help. She switched the selection to the thumb drive of music she liked. Most of it was country with a little soft rock. The two humans waited several minutes to watch and see how the dogs acted together and if they settled.

The music seemed to do the trick.

With the gang quiet, Gina and Tommy got off the floor and climbed over the fence. They sat on the smaller sofa, closest to the canine habitat they had constructed in the corner, in case they had to leap into action to save everyone from Pixie.

Despite it being mid-afternoon, the storm and overcast sky made it darker earlier than usual. Gina reached for the heavy quilt she used during the winter months and offered Tommy half of it. "Without the lights from the tree, it's a bit gloomy, isn't it?"

"I never put up a tree, but you're right. It makes the room cheery."

Her eyes widened. "You never put up a tree?"

He shook his head. "No, it seems like a waste and honestly, the holidays aren't all that special for me. It's a holiday made for sharing with kids. With a family. I prefer to work."

He stood and walked over to the fireplace, adding two more logs to the flames. He turned his back to the fire, glancing at the dogs before meeting Gina's eyes. "Growing up, Christmas was my least favorite time of the year, especially after Mom left us. We were off school, so we didn't have the benefit of the free lunch we could eat there. Then, there was the extra pressure of pretending we were excited about the break and holiday."

Gina stood and joined him at the hearth. "I'm sorry, Tommy. I wish we would have known. We could have done much more to help you and your brothers."

He shook his head and grinned. "Your family was always kind to us and the biggest reason we made it at all. Between your mom and Mabel at the café, we had food. Mabel and

Rusty gave Paul a job there washing dishes and cleaning and always sent him home with boxes of food they said they were getting ready to discard. Looking back, it was just their way of helping us without making it seem like we needed charity."

He sighed. "There was an old lady who lived in the trailer next to ours. I think she may have suspected we were on our own, but she never said a word. She kept to herself for the most part but would sometimes ask us for help lifting stuff or fixing small things. She used to bake us cakes on our birthdays. German chocolate was my favorite, and I remember that so vividly. Our mother never even acknowledged our birthdays, but this sweet little lady named Bernice always did."

Gina's heart ached for the man next to her. She could only imagine Tommy being fifteen and having the weight of the world on his shoulders and nobody to tell.

Nobody to help him.

Living in constant fear that if anyone learned the truth, they would be separated, had to have been stressful. He and Mike and Paul had banded together and hid their situation from everyone, putting on a brave front and staying under the radar.

He'd spent the last twenty-seven years being the adult, when he should have been able to still be a kid, at least for a few of them. Instead, he'd taken care of his brothers and took on the role that his parents had abdicated. Looking at the sorrow in his eyes, Gina understood, more than she ever had, Jo's quest to help the young people leaving the foster care system.

She reached for Tommy's hand and squeezed it in hers. His hand was warm and sturdy, his skin a bit rough. Tough, working hands like the man they belonged to. "For what it's worth, I think you did the right thing. I'm the oldest in our family and can't imagine being faced with the thought of splitting us apart and having to go to foster homes. I would have done the same thing, but I'm not sure I could have done it as well as you did." She whispered, "I can understand why Christmas is not the most wonderful time of the year for you. I'm sorry."

He squeezed her hand back. "It was a long time ago."

A gust of wind shook the house, and bushes scratched against the window, sending a shiver down Gina's spine. The dogs stirred; their ears perked. Seconds later, Pixie barked, and then Olive chimed in with a screechy yap.

Gina scowled at them and wandered into the kitchen. "I need a glass of wine. Do you want anything?"

"Something hot sounds good. I'm not much for wine."

A few minutes later, she carried in a plate stacked with cookies and a steaming mug of tea in one hand and her wine glass in the other. She set the plate on the end table and snuggled back into her half of the loveseat.

Tommy moved from his crouched position next to the dogs, where he had charmed the two now silent barkers and covered himself with the quilt before setting the plate of cookies between the two of them.

Gina took a sip from her glass and sighed. "I'm sure glad we have the fire; at least we get some light from it. I miss the twinkle lights from the tree." She glanced at the pile of dogs in the corner. "This is going to be a very strange Christmas."

Tommy finished chewing a cookie and smiled. "I've had worse."

CHAPTER 7

The hours of the storm wore on, with Gina and Tommy entertaining the dogs, sipping hot tea, and keeping the fire stoked. When it was time to feed the dogs their dinner, Tommy barricaded the smaller dogs and stayed with them in the living room, while Gina fed the others in the kitchen. Archie, like the other big dogs, got a sprinkling of the fruits and veggies Gina added to their food.

Once they were fed, she led them back to the living room and began the process of feeding the others. Olive, Pudge, and Pixie proved to be the most aggressive when it came to their food, so she left them and took Stubbs and Gonzo to the kitchen and fed them without a major incident.

She came back and found Tommy inside the wire with the three troublemakers and the big dogs on the outside watching him. She picked up Gonzo and Stubbs and handed them to Tommy.

Tommy chose Pudge next and handed her to Gina. "Careful, she's a heavyweight."

Gina cradled her in both arms. "I think I see where she

got her name." She looked down at her. "Okay, sweet girl, let's get you some dinner."

Once in the kitchen, she put Pudge down in front of the mat where she fed the dogs, and Pudge whined, clearly not in the mood to wait another minute for her meal. Gina chose her bowl from the three she had prepared and left on the counter.

Pudge gobbled her food in seconds, and Gina's forehead wrinkled. She needed to slow down when she ate. She made a mental note to look for one of the slow feeding bowls in her bin of samples.

Gina returned Pudge and picked up Olive, who was a slow eater. While she nibbled, Gina got Pixie and put her on the other side of the island to eat her dinner, out of view of Olive. It would take time to integrate the dogs eating together, and Gina was too tired to tackle that task.

While the girls finished their dinner, Gina wandered over to look out the window. She couldn't see much, but the pelting of snow against the window let her know the next trip outside with the dogs would be an undertaking.

Gina took the two tiniest of the group back to the living room and deposited them inside the wire. Tommy had left the enclosure to add another log to the fire.

"I'll take the big dogs out and come back for the others." He moved toward the kitchen. "I just need to bundle up."

"It looks horrible out there. Do you want me to come with you?"

He laughed. "There's no sense in both of us freezing. I'll be quick about it. I'm going to collect some of your solar lights and bring them indoors. We can use them for lights tonight and recharge them tomorrow. That will save our flashlights."

She nodded. "Good idea. Do you think you could check on Virginia while you're out?"

He pulled his beanie down over his ears. "Sure. I planned to go over and let the generator run for a bit, so they can turn on the furnace and make sure the fridge and freezer stay cool. I'll remind them to set an alarm clock, so they can keep the fire going. I'll go back in the morning to start it up again. I don't want to leave it running at night."

"Okay, I'll make some dinner while you get that done. I've got stuff for sandwiches, and I've got the soup I could heat up, but I'll have to open the refrigerator to get it."

"Works for me. I'll run the generator tonight, and we can make sure it's cooled back down, so if you need something in it, feel free. We'll just plan to run them long enough to warm up the house and cool down the fridge. That way we can conserve our fuel."

"Got it; that makes sense." She helped him leash the big dogs. Snow had a weird effect on them, like a stimulant. Tommy didn't need the hassle of chasing what amounted to dogs on crack through the snow-covered streets on a night like this one.

While Tommy took the experienced dogs, plus Archie outside, Gina retrieved plates from the cupboard and gathered the supplies she would need for dinner, including the soup. She added a generous amount to a shallow stainless-steel pot and set about making sandwiches by candlelight.

When she heard Tommy's boots stomping on the front steps, she attached the leashes to the other dogs' collars and steered them toward the back porch. To keep the two groups from getting overly excited and tangling their leashes together. Gina opted to use both porches—one for each group.

With that many dogs, she needed to be organized, or they'd run over the top of her.

Tommy placed a pile of solar yard lights on the floor of the porch, and she handed Tommy the leashes and scooted the dogs outside. Pixie and Olive weren't keen on the idea, both putting on the brakes as Tommy guided them outside. Pudge wasn't too happy either, with her low-slung tummy that was sure to get cold and wet in the snow. Gonzo and Stubbs were more curious and hopped down the steps, which left Tommy trying to coax the others without tugging on their leashes.

Gina left him to deal with the problem, taking a couple of the lights with her, and hurried to the front porch to begin the process of drying the big dogs. As she wiped their paws and removed snowballs from their long fur, she was reminded of all the times she had considered adopting a couple more dogs.

What had she been thinking? Even keeping up with four dogs was too much, but with eleven of them in the house, the trips outside took forever.

She finally finished the last paw and led the pack into the warm living room. They piled together in front of the fireplace, content to soak up the warmth of it and each other.

She washed her hands, thankful the city water was still flowing, and went back to her dinner prep. As she layered meat and cheese on the fluffy rolls, she grinned. They seemed like an unnecessary purchase at the time, but she was happy she'd added them to her cart at Costco.

The clomp of boots coming from the back door beckoned her with dry towels. Tommy herded the group of unruly dogs inside, all of them rushing to get out of the cold. Gina took a deep breath. "On your way to Virginia's, could you light the grill? I want to warm up the soup."

"Sure thing. I'll be back in a few." He disappeared around the corner of the house.

She tackled one dog at a time, starting with Gonzo, who was the most docile. He had the cutest grin, with his tiny, crooked teeth. She got him dried and removed his green sweater, before shutting the door on the others and carrying him to the living room pen and putting his sweater on the hearth to dry.

She hurried back and forth, drying and depositing each of them, adding to the row of colorful little sweaters on the hearth. They were much calmer after going outdoors and huddled together on top of the beds and blankets in search of warmth. With the dogs sorted, she bundled into her coat and stuck her feet in her boots, grabbing the pot of soup to take to the grill.

She'd never grilled soup before, so she wasn't sure how long it would take. She stayed on the porch with her wet boots, waiting. As she shivered, she hoped the power would come back on soon. She was better equipped than many but living like a modern pioneer woman was already getting old.

A cup of hot tea would be perfect right now, which prompted her to remember to boil more water. She slipped out of her boots and found another pot that would fit on the grill and filled it with water from the tap.

Careful not to jostle it too much, she carried it, a wooden spoon, and another solar light out to check the grill. She added the pot of water to the grate, gave the soup a stir, and touched the tip of the spoon to her tongue to test the temperature.

She wrinkled her nose. Lukewarm, at best. She shut the lid, turned up the flame, and scurried back indoors.

She continued to wait on the porch, checking her watch. Before ten minutes was up, Tommy appeared at the back door. "Virginia and the girls are fine. I'll go back after dinner to shut the generator off."

She handed him the spoon. "Could you check the soup and if the water is boiling, bring it in?"

"Will do. Hand me a towel so I can carry it in."

She shrugged off her boots. "I can grab you the oven mitts. That will be easier."

She dashed to the kitchen, retrieved a pair, and handed them through the door. "The soup wasn't quite warm enough when I checked it last."

He nodded and set off in quest of the rest of their dinner. While he was doing that, she pumped some water from the air pot. It was warm, but not hot enough for brewing tea. She poured it into a dishpan next to the sink and added some liquid soap.

Tommy banged on the back door, and she rushed to open it, holding it open while he carried in the pot of water. "Soup needs a little more time, but the water was boiling. I'm going to start your generator and let it run. That will keep your fridge cool and kick on the furnace to warm up the place."

She used another pair of mitts and took the pot from him, gingerly walking into the kitchen to put it on the stovetop. Pouring it into the air pot would be tricky. She didn't want to take a chance of spilling boiling water, so she found a large glass mixing bowl with a spout and poured into it first.

She filled the air pot and had enough left in the bowl to brew two cups of tea. Another tap on the back door sent her charging back to the porch to collect the pot of soup. She carried it to the kitchen, ladled two bowls from it, and added a bowl to each of their plates.

Once Tommy extracted himself from his layers of clothes, he joined her in the kitchen. While she added napkins and silverware, he hovered near the pot of soup, rubbing his hands together.

"This looks really good; thanks for making it."

"Hopefully, you like potato soup since we're getting a double dose of it today. It's one of my favorite comfort foods."

He picked up his plate and chuckled. "I'm not picky and

learned long ago never to turn down a meal. Until lately, I've never had to worry about gaining weight. All of us were lean. Now that I'm in my forties, I need to adjust and cut back a little. It's hard to change old habits."

They sat at the table in the dining room, where they could keep an eye on the dogs in the corner of the living room. Between the hot soup, tea, and the generator running the heating equipment, it was comfortable away from the fire.

Gina was still eating but noticed Tommy's plate and bowl were empty. "Would you like more?"

He patted his stomach. "I would, but I'm going to resist. Like I said, I need to dial back. This time of year is tough since almost everywhere I go, there are tempting treats, and our customers often drop off platters of cookies and boxes of candy."

She rolled her eyes. "I know. It's hard to behave during the holidays and in the winter, I don't get as much exercise. Otis and Watson hate that because they like nothing more than a couple of long walks each day. If they could walk a few hours and spend the other hours sleeping or sitting on my lap, their lives would be perfect."

Tommy chuckled. "Same with Zap. I've never been much of a gym guy. My work is physical for the most part, although I do spend a fair amount of time behind a desk. Zap would enjoy walking with other dogs. I can see she's enjoying being with them. Maybe we can make a pact to do that together in the new year. What do you think?"

She finished her last bite and nodded. "I like that idea. Having a friend to exercise with would make me more accountable. It's easy for me to talk myself out of a walk after a long day at work or sleep in when it's cold."

"We're always at the office early during the week. What time do you usually walk?"

"Well, it depends on the season. During the winter, it's

dark in the mornings, so some days I wait until I go downtown and walk them before the store opens. During the warmer seasons, I try to go early, around six thirty, before I get sidetracked with stuff for the store, the girls are usually still asleep, and the streets are quiet. If I'm behaving, I like to take the dogs for a second walk downtown after work. It's nice because the park is close, and the area is well-lit. Winter is tough with it getting dark so early and sunrise so late."

He nodded and followed her into the kitchen to deposit the dirty dishes in the sudsy water. "We could definitely do the after-work route with you, and some mornings might work for us. I'm usually at work by seven, but I could take a break and meet you at the store before you open."

"That sounds like a plan." She poured the leftover soup back into a container and put it in the fridge.

Tommy wandered to the back porch and bundled into his outerwear and boots. "I'll head out to turn off Virginia's generator and do one more check over there, and then I'll shut down yours."

"Sounds good. Then when you get back, we can finish off the evening with a fun wrestling activity." He frowned, and she chuckled. "I like to call it try to put the dry sweaters back on the dogs." He laughed and went through the door.

She remembered the partial bottle of white wine she had stashed in the fridge and hurried to retrieve it. She'd need a glass after redressing the dogs and if need be, she could stick it outside to keep it chilled.

She caught herself thinking of Tommy while she was rubbing a towel across a plate she had already dried. He was so genuine. Not like some of the guys her friends had tried to set her up with after the divorce.

Slimy was the best word she could think of to describe most of them.

They all pretended to be something they weren't.

Tommy wasn't like that.

Not having dated in years and being so busy with the girls and her business, she hadn't missed male companionship. Or, at least that's what she thought.

Tommy sparked a flutter of interest she hadn't experienced in a long time and hadn't expected. If she had to be stranded by a blizzard and a blackout, she couldn't ask for better company.

CHAPTER 8

Monday morning, an unusual sound woke Gina from where she had sprawled on the loveseat the night before. She shivered and looked to see only glowing embers in the fireplace. She gritted her teeth.

She had been on duty and had fallen asleep. She would have never survived as a pioneer woman.

She untangled the quilt and extra blanket she was wrapped in and hurried to spread the coals and add a couple of dry logs. She blew on the embers, hoping the logs would ignite and after a few tries, she was rewarded with yellow flames. She blew out a long breath. How could she have let this happen?

She slept until two in the morning and didn't think she was that tired. She looked over at the couch and couldn't even see Tommy under the mountain of blankets that covered him.

She willed the fire to get roaring so she could add more wood before he woke. She looked over in the corner, where all the dogs were huddled together in a pile. After their last trip outside, she and Tommy had put them all together inside the makeshift fence last night.

As she watched the flames lick the logs, she remembered the weird sound that woke her. She concentrated on listening and heard it again. Sort of a scratching sound.

Maybe the wind was causing something to scrape against the porch. She looked outside and noticed trees were no longer swaying, and there was only a gentle shower of snow falling in the glow of the streetlight. She kept a blanket wrapped around her shoulders and listened again, trying to pinpoint the location. It was coming from the other side of the room, where the tree was.

Picturing a critter in the tree, she got goosebumps, hoping it was friendly. She couldn't see very well in the dark corner, so she tiptoed over by the front door and snatched up one of the solar lights that was still glowing.

Armed with her weak light in one hand and the other at her chest, keeping the blanket around her, she skulked toward the tree.

She eyed the branches but didn't see anything amiss. As she moved the solar light lower, she caught the glint of a reflection and peered closer.

As her eyes focused, a high-pitched bark greeted her.

Pixie.

Gina set the light on the floor and got down on her stomach, stretching her arms out so she could extract the troublemaker from her hiding spot behind the presents. She finally got her hands around the dog and pulled her out under the branches at the front of the tree.

Gina rolled over and brought Pixie to her chest. That's when she noticed a ripped piece of wrapping paper caught on the dog's tooth. When she reached up to remove it, she was met with a snarl.

"Oh, you're a naughty one." Gina stood her ground and

snagged the soggy paper from her mouth. She carried her to the other side of the room and put her inside the fence.

She added a larger log to the fire, making a loud clunk. Tommy stirred at the noise, and his head popped up from under the blankets.

"Sorry," she whispered.

"It's fine. I need to get up anyway." He squinted and looked at his watch. "It's after six."

"We have an escape artist on our hands. I just found Pixie behind the tree, ripping up packages."

He chuckled. "She's a handful, isn't she? Tiny in stature, but a huge personality."

Together, they investigated the wire enclosure. They found nothing amiss, but where the wire panel met each wall, they realized it wouldn't take much to push on it and create a small opening.

Tommy nodded as he surveyed the dogs. "I think she had an accomplice."

Gina was busy counting and making sure all the shelter dogs were there. Olive was the other tiny one that could get through a small space, but she was there snuggled next to Archie.

"Do you think one of the big dogs let her climb onto his back, and she scaled the fence?" Gina laughed as she imagined it.

"That's a definite possibility. More likely, one of the big dogs could have fallen asleep against the end of the panel and inadvertently pushed it to create a small gap. Then not one to let an opportunity go to waste, Pixie climbed on top of him and squeezed out through the space."

"Makes sense." She studied the dogs. All of them gave her their best doe-eyed looks of innocence. "I guess we need some security cameras installed in here just to keep track of this ragtag crew."

"I'll get my gear on and take them outside. Then I'll get the generators going, and we can get this place warmed up a bit." He gave Zap a quick scratch behind the ears and headed to the porch.

Gina inspected the packages under the tree and discovered Pixie had chewed the corners off three of them. She pulled the damaged boxes out and set them on the dining room table. She'd have to rewrap the gifts for Ollie and Grace.

As she gave it more thought, she removed all the gifts from under the tree and stacked them on the table. She didn't need any more trouble. Once the roads were passable, she could run up to the store and get another set of wire panels and cordon off the tree.

She loved dogs and had a special place in her heart for any of them in a shelter, but she couldn't keep doing this and keep her store running. She hoped the part to fix whatever was wrong at the shelter wouldn't be delayed too long.

It was only two days until Christmas. This was one of her busiest days of the year, and she needed the revenue. All the downtown merchants would feel the pinch of fewer customers because of the storm.

Tommy shoveled the walkways again and then came to collect the first group of dogs. He handed her a notice that had been stuck in the porch door.

She opened it and found a memo from the city, letting residents know the water supply was in jeopardy, and they didn't expect power to be restored soon. They asked residents to conserve as much as possible and be prepared. The community center and the high school were both open and were running on emergency power. They had supplies, including food and water, for those who needed assistance.

Once the high winds and the worst of the storm was over, crews would begin repairs and restore the power and cell service, but it wouldn't be soon. The road conditions also made it impossible for deliveries of supplies to reach their little mountain town, so the mayor urged neighbors to help neighbors.

Gina's hopes for the power coming on soon were dashed. By the time they completed the leashing, drying, and unleashing of the dogs, Gina was dreaming of a hot bubble bath and a glass of wine.

At this point, just being able to boil water would be a reason to celebrate. Operating with little sleep and lacking the normal conveniences she relied on each day began to wear on her.

She scolded herself as she prepared breakfast for the dogs. People had suffered through far worse things.

It was only a severe winter storm.

Wouldn't be the first.

Or the last.

Nothing was permanent. Nothing would last forever.

Her mom always reminded her of that. When things were tough during her divorce, her mom would call and remind her of it.

When she moved back home and had to deal with two surly teenagers, her mom would make her tea and listen to her woes, reminding her again that things wouldn't be the same forever.

That meant the good and the bad, so she needed to relax and go with the flow. The sun would shine again. That was her dad's favorite saying.

She wrote off being on edge and a little cranky to neglecting her duties and then being startled awake. She was thankful Tommy was there and was such a big help.

Not having a cooking device indoors was cumbersome. She would never again take for granted the ability to brew coffee or boil water for tea.

Her agitated state was a clear sign she was addicted to caffeine or at least the ritual of her morning cup of warmth.

If only she had opted for a gas stove when she remodeled, she could have boiled all the water she wanted, but she had chosen the electric one with the easy to clean top. She could almost hear Luke's voice recommending the gas. He was right.

The purr of the generator was followed by the welcomed sound of the heater blowing warm air throughout the house.

Tommy poked his head through the open back door and asked her to bring him the solar lights so he could put them outside to recharge.

She dashed into the living room, gathered them up, and then went about feeding her hungry pack. She was just finishing with the last of them when Tommy rattled the back door, and she saw the steaming pot of water in his hands.

Knowing a hot cup of tea was only minutes away brought a smile to her face. She grabbed the potholders and hurried to carry the pot to the stovetop. Tommy took his mug outside so he could finish shoveling in the backyard and turn off Virginia's generator.

With the dogs fed and safely back in their enclosure, Gina contemplated breakfast. The lack of cookware suitable for the grill gave her pause. Then she remembered the aluminum foil pans she had in the pantry.

With the flashlight in hand, she scanned the shelves in the dark pantry and found them. She gathered frozen hashbrowns, eggs, some ham lunchmeat, shredded cheese, a tomato, and green onions. She set the hashbrowns on the hearth to thaw while she whipped the eggs and diced the ham, tomato, and onions.

Her teacup was empty, so she brewed another and collected the thawed hashbrowns, adding them and the ham to the pan. She mixed the veggies and cheese into the eggs and poured it into the pan. She covered the pan with foil and carried it to the back porch.

She caught Tommy's eye and handed him the pan. "Indirect heat should work and check it in about thirty minutes. It will probably need more, but I don't want to chance burning it."

He gave her a mock salute and left with a smile.

The casserole was too much for the two of them. She eyed the dogs and told the four that usually minded her, she'd be right back, leaving them in charge of the others. She slipped into her jacket and boots and headed across the front lawn to Virginia's house.

The door opened slightly, revealing a wary brown eye. Then the door swung wider, and Jillian greeted her with a smile.

"We haven't had any visitors, so I wondered who it could be." Her brown eyes widened as she pointed at the tall pine tree covered in snow. "It's just beautiful with the snow covering everything, isn't it? Like one of those pretty Christmas cards with the glitter."

Gina nodded and handed her the envelope from the city that had been wedged in Virginia's door. "It's from the city, letting us know the water is likely to go out, and they'll be working to restore things once the worst of the storm is over."

The young woman took the envelope. "I'll let Virginia know, and we'll fill a few more jugs."

"What I came to tell you is we're making a breakfast casserole, and it should be ready in less than an hour. We'll deliver it when it's ready; that way you girls won't have to make breakfast today. I know it's not easy without a working stovetop."

Jillian's brows arched. "Oh, that would be great. We were just going to have some cereal or granola bars."

"I need to get back and check on the dogs, but I'll send it over as soon as it's ready."

"If you need help with the dogs, I'd love to sit with them."

Gina chuckled. "I might take you up on that." She turned to go and waved goodbye, stepping into the tracks she had left in the deep snow.

Once she got to her walkway, which was cleared thanks to Tommy, she gripped the porch rail and tapped her boots against the edge of the steps to remove the snow. She slipped out of them and left them in the entryway to dry before making for the fireplace to warm her hands.

She gazed at the unlit tree in the corner. Gina's worry about being alone during the holidays had disappeared, but Christmas would be nothing like the past. Tomorrow was Christmas Eve, and her hope of keeping with her tradition of making ravioli dimmed by the minute.

She took a deep breath and stood straighter. She had to come to terms with the fact that she would have to delay her traditional meal until the power was restored and her kitchen was in working order. She had some steaks in the freezer and if all else failed, they could grill them for a holiday meal.

Tommy's comment that he'd had worse Christmases stuck with her. She had nothing to complain about.

With her hands toasty again, she wandered over to the enclosure to pet the dogs. "This is one weird Christmas, isn't it?" As she talked to each of them, stroking their ears or scratching their chins, her anxiety disappeared.

"I wish the girls were here, but it's probably better that I don't have to worry about them. You guys are enough of a handful, aren't you?"

Dogs were the best therapists.

She frowned as her eyes darted between the dogs. She

didn't see Pixie. She looked again, picking up all the dog beds to search under them and the blankets.

No Pixie.

Gina's head throbbed. "Where could that little rascal be?" In her rushing between the front and back porch, she had forgotten to secure the gate across the door that led to the dining room and kitchen.

Her heart sank. She didn't want anything to happen to Pixie. She called for Otis and Watson to come and let them roam through the house, knowing they had a better chance of locating her quickly.

In her happy voice, she called out Pixie's name as she wandered through the kitchen and the hallway along it. Her door and Luke's door were closed, so she couldn't have gotten too far, if she went exploring.

Gina moved to the back porch and gasped when she saw the door wasn't quite closed. "Oh, no."

She rushed back to get her boots and put on her coat and gloves. She motioned Otis and Watson to wait by the back door, trusting their noses to help her find the renegade.

She kept her eyes focused on the ground, looking for tiny paw prints in the snow, as she rounded the house and found Tommy near the generator.

"Pixie has escaped. I didn't see her in the house, and the back door didn't quite latch, so I'm worried she's out here somewhere."

Tommy stood from his crouched position next to the generator. "I haven't seen her come by here. I've had the gate open but been right here, so I think I would have noticed her."

Gina's throat burned, and her heart pounded in her chest.

He reached his gloved hands toward hers. "Don't worry. We'll find her."

"I thought Otis and Winston might have a better shot at finding her. They're waiting by the back door."

He nodded. "Let's look across the grass before we let them trample it. We might see her paw prints in the snow. Her sweater is black and pink, right?"

Gina nodded and turned to scout the perimeter of the backyard. It was fenced, so Pixie should be confined to the yard, but with the side gate open to the breezeway, she couldn't be sure.

Gina also couldn't imagine the dog venturing into the deep snow. She'd be sure to see body-sized prints. She and Tommy searched the yard, paying close attention to the bushes and plants along the fence line and had no luck spotting Pixie.

Worry overwhelmed Gina. She couldn't handle it if something happened to the little dog.

The casserole was ready to come off the grill, and Tommy suggested she take it inside. He'd search the front of the house, just in case the dog managed to get by him while he had the side gate open.

She trudged back to the house, carrying their hot breakfast. Balancing the pan, she slipped out of her boots and carried it into the kitchen. After cutting the casserole into generous squares, she placed half of it in a container.

It smelled and looked delicious, but her appetite was gone. Her stomach, in knots, lurched as she contemplated Pixie's fate. She'd never forgive herself if she were lost or hurt.

She took the container and slipped back into her boots, keeping her eye out for any sign of Pixie as she went around the side of the house. Tommy's head was down, focused on the ground as he continued the search in the front yard.

Gina hurried to the front door of Virginia's house and handed the hot breakfast to Morgan, who answered the door this time. "Oh, that looks yummy," she said. "Thanks for thinking of us."

Her forehead creased slightly as she looked closer at Gina. "Are you okay?"

Gina shook her head. "Not really. One of the shelter dogs, Pixie, escaped somehow. She's a tiny Yorkie, and she's wearing a pink and black sweater. If you happen to see her, please let me know."

"Oh, I'm sorry. We'll keep an eye out. I hope you find her."

Gina waved goodbye, not trusting her voice to say anything further. She scanned the snow-covered yard but only saw her own tracks in the snow from her trips back and forth to her neighbor.

Tommy's head lifted when she reached the front walkway. He shook his head. "No luck. No tracks, nothing." He looked up at the house. "Let's go in and search the house again, just to make sure. Pixie doesn't like the snow, so I can't imagine she'd be out here and not yiping."

He pointed to the side gate. "I'll make one more pass in the back and meet you inside."

Gina's shoulders sagged as she climbed the steps to the front porch. Pixie was vocal, so what he said made sense. She stomped the snow from her boots and bent down to slip out of them before opening the door to the house.

"Aaak," she said as she stepped into a small puddle with only her sock on her foot.

She reached into the basket with the towels and quickly pulled her hand back. Then she peered closer and moved some of the towels, revealing the little fur-covered girl they had been searching for everywhere.

Gina lifted Pixie from the nest she had burrowed amid the towels. The dog was perfectly happy, not shaking, and didn't seem to have a care in the world. Gina brought Pixie to her neck and rested her chin atop the dog's tiny head.

"You had me scared to death, little miss." She hugged her tighter. "I'm so glad you're okay, even though part of me wants to give your little bum a good spanking."

She carried Pixie inside and sat on the hearth in front of the fire with her.

Minutes later, Tommy came into the living room. He did a double-take when he spotted her sitting on the hearth.

"You found her. Where was the little scoundrel?"

Gina told him about the basket of towels on the front porch. "I'm not sure when she scooted out there, but I'm glad she's not lost."

He joined her on the hearth, sitting close enough that their thighs touched. He reached out and petted the top of Pixie's head. "You're a naughty little brat. A cute one, but still a brat."

CHAPTER 9

※

After getting through another dinner, the process of running the generators, and taking the dogs out for their final visit of the evening, Gina and Tommy had stayed up late last night playing cards and board games until the wee hours of the morning. The stress of losing Pixie had drained them and being a huge fan of games and cards, Gina had suggested they pass some time playing.

She taught Tommy how to play canasta and gin rummy, and they played several games of Scattegories. Some of Gina's favorite memories revolved around family games. Introducing and sharing them with Tommy was an evening well spent.

He hadn't played many games growing up and from the smile on his face, Gina was sure he'd also enjoyed it. They drank hot tea and snacked on cookies as they played, making for a festive evening in front of the fire.

They had made sure the gates were secure in case anybody decided to follow in Pixie's pawprints, before turning in for the evening. He took the couch, and she opted for the recliner. They stoked the fire, and both went to sleep.

Before the sun even considered rising, Gina woke and blinked a few times, not believing her eyes.

In the corner of the living room, her Christmas tree was lit up with the hundreds of lights she and Luke had strung on it. She checked the lamp on the end table and found it was still off. That was the one item she left plugged in, so they'd know when the power had been restored.

What was going on? She slipped out of the recliner, taking care to be as quiet as possible. The fire was still burning but could use a log or two. She elected to wait and slipped across the wooden floor to investigate.

With it being so dark, she couldn't see well but searched around near the bottom of the tree where she knew her controller was plugged into the wall outlet. She found a small box with the master plug inserted into an outlet on it.

A piece of electrical tape held a page from the notepad she had used to keep score with last night. She pulled off the paper and held it closer to the tree lights. She turned it to make out the blocky lettering.

MERRY CHRISTMAS, GINA. I HOPE THE LIGHTS MAKE YOUR HOLIDAY BRIGHTER—TOMMY.

She held the paper close to her chest and gazed at the tree. He had given her the perfect gift. She remembered mentioning how much she loved the lights and was touched that he had listened. Even more impressive was that he had tried to fix them.

She only wished she could think of an equally meaningful gift for him. With the stores closed, she'd have to come up with something she already had at the house. The pressure was on because she was sure she couldn't top this.

It had been a long time since a man, who wasn't related to her, had done something so thoughtful. Don had been attentive when they were first together, but that aspect of their marriage had faded over the years.

She had fallen for his charm and good looks, so much so that now she was wary of handsome men. She shouldn't punish them, since they weren't all the same, and they couldn't help the fact that she'd been too naïve to recognize Don's arrogance and self-absorption. They had been happy when she was young and equally stunning, but as the years went by, his eyes wandered elsewhere.

She kept trying to make things work for the sake of her kids. When she finally got brave enough to begin divorce proceedings, he used the girls as a wedge. All of that had driven her home into the arms of her parents and the loving community of Granite Ridge.

Tommy stirred and pulled the quilt higher. That's when she noticed Pixie snuggled into his shoulder. That little charmer must have batted her tiny eyelashes at him last night, and he let her sleep with him. He was quite the soft touch.

She moved to the hearth and added two logs, taking great care to place them without making much noise. She then sat on the hearth, admiring the tree. Otis and Watson watched her from the pile of dogs but snuggled back with the others as soon as she sat.

The flames curled around the new logs and warmed her back. Sleeping in the recliner made her neck stiff, so the heat helped loosen her muscles. She glanced over at the snoozing dogs, willing them to stay quiet. If she started moving around, she'd disturb them, and the chaos would begin.

It wasn't like she had anything to do. No power meant fewer chores. She thought about the laundry she had intended to wash. That made her wonder how the pioneers had accomplished washing clothes in the winter. That would have been an overwhelming job.

Her mind raced with what they could make to go with their grilled steaks, then she glimpsed the lights on the tree.

Instead of worrying about it, she tiptoed back to the recliner, snuggled under her quilt, and soaked in the tree. She would never again underestimate the power of twinkle lights.

They elicited fond memories of her childhood and the years when her girls were young, their faces filled with the wonder of the season. Nothing would ever top that feeling she had when they would rush to the tree on Christmas morning, eyes wide with excitement.

The lights weren't just pretty. They were a symbol of all the good things about the Christmases past and hope for those in the future. She loved nothing more than getting up early and sipping her first cup of coffee while enjoying them.

No coffee today, but she wouldn't let that dampen the joy she felt as she looked upon the tree.

The peace and quiet of the early morning lasted almost an hour before Tommy stirred and woke. In moving, he dislodged Pixie and was greeted with a couple of quick yaps.

He turned his head and said, "Morning."

"Good morning to you. I've just been sitting here enjoying my Christmas gift. I love the lights. Not sure how you did that without me hearing you."

He grinned. "I'm glad you like it. That little power box won't run them for long, but I wanted to surprise you."

"I love them."

She gestured at Pixie. "Looks like somebody conned you into letting her out of the pen last night."

He looked at the tiny dog. "When I was setting up the lights, she barked once, and I was afraid she'd wake you, so I carried her around and then was afraid if I put her back, she'd start her yapping."

As if she knew what he had said, Pixie yipped.

That set off the others, who no doubt were miffed that she had received special treatment. Pudge and Olive protested with whines and barks, while the others looked at them and became agitated. Stubbs paced the perimeter of the enclosure.

It was time to take them outside.

She left her warm cocoon and went to gather their leashes. Tommy bundled into his jacket and boots and met her on the back porch, after starting the generator. With the little dogs outside, Gina fixed breakfast for all the dogs and had time to feed the big ones before Tommy returned with the others.

Once they were fed, she attached their leashes and staged them in the living room. The tap on the back porch door signaled the return of the small dogs. After Pixie's shenanigans, the other dogs weren't allowed out the front door.

She made sure the door to the kitchen was closed and then hurried to the front of the house to hand off the bigger dogs to Tommy. Since they'd been fed, and the snow had stopped falling, Tommy could take them on a longer walk.

That gave her plenty of time to get back to the porch, dry everyone off, take off their sweaters, and leave them by the fire to go about feeding them. Pixie and Olive were still not trustworthy when it came to group feeding, so they waited in the enclosure while the others ate.

The slow feeding bowl was working, and Pudge wasn't the first to gulp down her breakfast. Gonzo and Stubbs finished before her, and they got some belly rubs and ear scratches while they waited for her to finish.

As soon as Pixie and Olive ate, Tommy arrived at the back porch with his charges. He handed her the leashes through the door. "I'm going to do a bit of shoveling here and at Virginia's. Then I'll turn off both generators."

She nodded. "Not sure what you want for breakfast. I've got cereal."

He wrinkled his nose. "How about a sandwich?"

She laughed. "Why not? I'll get these hooligans dried off and make them."

"If you leave a pot of water on the step, I'll get it boiling and holler at you when it's ready."

"Will do. It'll be after I get these guys settled."

She went about the laborious task of wiping six sets of paws and settling them on their beds near the fire, which needed another log.

With that done, she made sure the gate was secured across the living room doorway, carried the pot of water to the back steps, and then went about gathering supplies to make sandwiches. She could kill for an actual breakfast sandwich right now but would have to settle for a cold one.

As she went about layering the meat and cheese, she contemplated their dinner menu. Potatoes on the grill would make the most sense and be the easiest side dish to accompany their steaks. She could slice up potatoes, add cheese and onions, and put them in foil to cook on the grill.

She added the sandwiches to plates, along with some apple slices, and set them on the dining room table.

The rattle of the porch door caught her attention, and she swiped the oven mitts as she hurried to the door.

Tommy held the steaming pot in front of him. "Virginia's place is done. I'll just finish up here. Should only be about ten minutes."

She completed the transfer of the boiling water into the air pot and set two cups of tea to brew.

While she waited, she visited her bathroom and tidied her hair, which had become loose from the hair tie she used to hold her ponytail. As she fiddled with her hair, she glanced at her shower. She'd love nothing more than a steaming shower and a chance to wash her hair.

Maybe tomorrow.

She checked on the dogs, who were relatively calm, with some chewing on toys and others almost asleep.

As she removed the tea bags, Tommy came through the back door. "Whew, I'm ready for breakfast."

She motioned her head toward the dining room. "I've got sandwiches ready, and here's a nice mug of tea."

As they ate, she shared her idea of potatoes to go with their steaks. He popped an apple slice into his mouth and nodded. "That sounds perfect to me."

"When the power comes on, you have to promise me you'll come over and make ravioli with me. It's a family tradition, and it's so delicious. I would normally be doing that today."

"You don't need to twist my arm when there's food involved. I'll be here, no matter what day it is."

As they finished their unconventional breakfast, part of Gina hoped the power wouldn't be restored until after Christmas. She'd miss out on all her normal cooking and baking traditions, but she'd extend Tommy's stay.

Having him here had made the lonely Christmas she had anticipated rather fun. She hated the inconvenience but hated the idea of Tommy leaving more.

CHAPTER 10

They went about their new daily routines of making sure the solar lights were outside to charge and washing the dishes in the pans of leftover water from the air pot, with Tommy stacking more wood when he went out to shut down the generator.

When he came in after taking the dogs out again, he pointed at the sky. "Check it out. It looks like things are clearing up. That's a good sign we might get power back soon. They'll be able to get to work on it now that the storm has cleared."

She smiled, hoping to hide the sliver of disappointment that crept in at the thought of being alone again. "Being able to cook and take a shower would be wonderful."

He laughed and swiped a cookie from the plate she had left on the granite counter. "I agree. The downside is, I'll probably be inundated with calls from customers. I need to check on the part for the shelter as soon as we can use the computer. The storm delayed deliveries and now with Christmas…" He squinted as he studied the calendar on the fridge. "I bet it won't be here before Friday at the earliest." He sighed and added, "So, I'm afraid you'll be stuck with the dogs and me until we can get the shelter up and running."

He winked, and something fluttered in her chest. It blossomed into warmth and traveled throughout her body, all the way to her toes that curled inside her fluffy socks.

Was it bad that she was secretly glad the part would be delayed? "If not for the last few days with them, I would have said, don't worry, I can handle them, but there's no way. It's a two-person job at minimum."

He laughed. "They are more than a handful, aren't they? Especially the little purse-sized ones."

A chill made Gina shiver. She got up and brewed two more cups of tea, cradling her cup in her hands. "Let's go sit by the fire. I'm already starting to get cold."

He took his mug and the plate of cookies and followed.

She nodded at the table they had used to play games. "How about we try Yahtzee today?"

As they rolled the dice and shared in the excitement of Tommy rolling out a Yahtzee on his first game, Gina remembered about her dinner date with Leslie. "So, on Thursday, the day after Christmas, I'm meeting Leslie up at Cedar Mountain Lodge for dinner. Do you think you'll be okay to stay and watch the dogs on your own?"

He grinned as he added his latest score to the pad. "I'm sure I'll manage. We'll have power by then, so it will make things easier."

She laughed and added, "Right, I guess we won't be going anywhere if the power is out. I hate leaving you, but I promised her."

He waved off her concern with a flash of his hand. "Not a problem. I'm happy to stay. She's on my list of customers to visit after the holidays. She's looking to do some upgrades in the old barn."

Gina's brows rose. "I'm surprised she came back to

Granite Ridge. I know that was a big part of the reason she and Eric got divorced. She didn't want to leave Seattle."

"I wondered how that was working out with her coming back and Eric being such a part of the community. With him being the fire chief and involved in so many things, it's probably hard for her to avoid him."

Gina clapped and whooped as she pointed at the Yahtzee that tumbled out of the cup. "I haven't talked to her much since she came back this fall. I went to her dad's funeral and have seen her downtown a couple of times. I'm sure I'll get the whole story Thursday. She's always been a talker."

Tommy laughed. "Eric's a good guy. Hopefully, they can get along."

"I remember being excited to get out of here, go somewhere bigger, more exciting. Maybe now that she's older, and her mom needs her help, she'll be more content here. I know I'm happy to be back home."

"I've never had the desire to go to a bigger place or a city. I like the familiar places and faces in Granite Ridge. I'd never survive in a city. Each time I go to Boise, the traffic makes me crazy."

She nodded. "I like the slower pace here. Not to mention being near my parents, Luke, and now his new family. With my girls leaving home soon, I can't imagine being anywhere else."

As lunchtime approached, they readied the dogs for a trip outdoors. Gina walked out onto the back porch and gasped. They'd been so busy with their game, they hadn't noticed the sun shining brightly in the pale-blue sky.

"It's gorgeous outside. I'm going with you. Maybe we can take the dogs on a longer walk. That sunshine gives me hope."

She stuffed her hair inside her hat and slipped into her

boots. "I'll let you wrangle the small ones. I think the others will be easier for me to handle, even though they're big."

He chuckled and took hold of the leashes. "They look harmless, but I think you're right."

They headed out the front door and guided the dogs down the walkway, cleared and already beginning to dry in the warmth of the sun. People around the neighborhood were outside, shoveling snow from their driveways and sidewalks.

Snowmen and entire snow families decorated several yards. People gawked and waved at the two of them, no doubt taken in by the herd of dogs they attempted to control.

Gina led the way with three dogs tethered in each hand. They all loved the snow and kept trying to nip at the piles along the edge of the walkways. Her goldens liked nothing more than to dive into a pile and get a snout full of snow. Tunneling was their favorite winter activity.

She kept a firm rein on them, hoping they wouldn't be a bad influence on Archie, who followed their every move. The streets were still covered in snow with only a few tracks from people who had braved them. There was nowhere to go but being stuck inside made some people stir crazy.

They made a big loop through the residential area, where Gina often walked Otis and Watson, and encountered only a few sidewalks still packed with deep snow. Finn and Zap, with Hank on one side, attacked the mounds of snow, making body-sized trenches through it.

Tommy laughed. "They should get a job with the snow plow service." It worked out well for the smaller dogs who weren't as enamored with the white stuff and scurried through the ruts the others had made without getting buried in the drifts.

By the time they returned to the house, Gina was ready for

a break. She led her charges through the side gate and let them loose in the backyard. They needed to run off some energy and would get their fill of burrowing through the snow.

Tommy followed with the smaller dogs, and Gina helped to get them onto the back porch. He pointed to the door. "I'll turn on the generator so we can get the house warmed up and get the dogs dried."

"Sounds good. I'll get their sweaters off and set them to dry." Pudge was the first one she dried. She was completely docile, probably having never walked that far in a long time. Gina carried her and her orange sweater into the living room, where the dog sank into her bed.

Gina had to wrestle with Pixie and Olive to remove their sweaters. They were both beyond wiggly after the walk and nipped at her the entire time she was drying them. She was happy to put them in the pen and get away from their sharp teeth.

Gonzo and Stubbs were cooperative, and Gonzo had even begun lifting his paws for the toweling-off routine. Gina booped his nose and told him he was a good dog before removing his blue sweater. He and Stubbs both followed her into the living room like well-behaved dogs, and she lifted them over the fence.

After she lined up all the sweaters on the hearth, Gina stood in front of the fire and warmed her hands.

With it being well after the lunch hour, she considered what they could fix for a meal. With steak on the menu for dinner, something light would be best. She stepped into the kitchen as Tommy returned from outside.

She drummed her fingers on the counter. "How would you feel about cheese and crackers, some fruit, maybe some chips and salsa, for lunch? I'm thinking more like snacks since we'll be having a big dinner."

"Fine by me. I'll eat anything." He moved to the counter and pumped hot water from the air pot into his cup.

With the furnace warming the house, they ate at the counter in the kitchen. They were gathering the plates to wash when the hum of the refrigerator startled them.

Tommy grinned. "Power's back on." He hurried to the porch. "I'll turn off your generator, check on Virginia and the girls, and head out to your dad's to shut his down."

He reached into his pocket and turned on his cell phone, having chosen to turn it off and keep it charged as much as possible. His brows rose. "We have service."

"That's great news," said Gina. "I can't wait to get started on some chores like my pile of laundry." She eyed her coffee machine on her counter. "I might even brew a pot of coffee. Tea was easier to deal with, but I've missed it."

Tommy chuckled as he slipped on his boots. He whistled for Zap, who came running from her place with the big dogs in the living room. Hank followed her, having taken quite a liking to his new friend and not as well trained as the others, who remained on their beds.

Gina bent down and stroked his head. "You've got to stay here with me, little buddy. Zap will be back soon."

Tommy turned before going out the door. "Do you need anything while I'm out?"

Gina's forehead creased. "If you have time, could you go by my shop and turn off the trickle of water I left going and make sure the heat's on?" She extracted the shop keys from her purse.

"Sure, not a problem." He took the keyring, slipping it into his pocket where he kept her dad's keys. "I'll be back as soon as I can. I want to stop by my shop and see if there's an update on my parts order. If you think of anything else, just call my cell."

Gina waved as he and Zap headed outside. She used her

electric coffee grinder, and the rich aroma made her smile. She added the ground beans and water to the coffee machine and hit the brew button.

She took Hank back into the living room and noticed the lights on her tree were dark. She unplugged them from the power box Tommy had used and plugged them back into the wall outlet. The tree lit up and so did the smile on her face.

After a cup of fresh coffee, her bathroom was warmed, and she hopped in the shower, delighted to languish under the spray and wash her hair. After dressing in fresh jeans and a warm turtleneck, she enjoyed another cup of coffee and sat in front of the fire, letting her hair dry.

As much as she'd like to get her living room in order, she couldn't bear the thought of moving the dogs back to the porch. They were too accustomed to being part of the activity and would be sad out there all alone.

More than anything, she needed to get started making ravioli. She threw in a load of clothes to wash and gathered the ingredients. As she worked, she poured herself a glass of wine, since that was the Turner family's first rule of making ravioli.

Her cell phone rang, and she wiped her hands to answer it, smiling at Luke's name on the screen.

"Hey, I was just calling to check on things after seeing the weather reports up there. How are you?"

She laughed. "You wouldn't believe it if I told you." She gave him a brief recap of the last few days and how eleven dogs and Tommy came to stay with her throughout the storm. "Tommy's out at Dad's checking on the generator and my shop. He's going to stay until we can get the dogs back to the shelter."

"I'm glad everything's okay there. I'm also glad we're in sunny California right now." She heard voices in the background. "Dad says thanks for taking care of his place. How are my boys?"

She assured him Finn and Hank were doing well and told him she had delayed making ravioli, but was starting the process now that she had power. She promised to pick them up at the airport on Sunday.

"I'm glad you're not alone at Christmas, Gina. I hated leaving you there and am glad you have company."

She glanced at the pile of dogs in the corner. "I've got plenty of company. I'll see you in five days." She disconnected after he put her on speakerphone so everyone could wish her a Merry Christmas.

She went back to prepping the dough and making the filling, along with one other special surprise. She turned on her favorite Christmas tunes and went to work. By the time Tommy and Zap returned, she had several sheets of the savory pillows of dough prepared and ready for cooking.

While he was still in his boots and jacket, he took the dogs outside, letting the big dogs roam on their own in the backyard after taking out the smaller group. Once he got all their paws dried, he herded and carried the bunch into the living room, then tackled the larger breeds.

With all the dogs nestled in the living room and the fire stoked, he came back into the kitchen and lifted his nose.

The butter sauce, along with the tomatoey meat sauce she had made filled the house with an inviting scent, and Tommy stretched his neck to get a look at what was on the stovetop. "Something smells mighty good."

She lifted her head from the sheets of ravioli. "This year, I'm making pumpkin with butter sauce and walnuts and just the traditional cheese with a meat sauce." She pointed at the hook next to the fridge. "Grab an apron, and you can help."

He washed his hands and slipped the apron over his neck.

"I'm not that great in the kitchen when it comes to fancy stuff. It might be better if I just watched."

She waved her hand. "Nah, it's easy, I promise." She took a sip from her wine glass. "First rule is you have to have a glass of wine while you cook these."

He wrinkled his nose. "I'll pass on that. I may end up getting called out, so I'll stick with that coffee you promised."

She showed him how to spoon the topping onto the sheets of pasta and use the cutter to slice the dough. He caught on quickly and let her know all was well at her shop and her dad's place as they worked together to finish the last of the dough.

"Sorry we were gone so long; I had a few customers with problems and stopped by to help them. Nothing major, thank goodness."

"Any news on the part for the shelter?" Gina asked, as she gave the sauce a quick stir.

"They're closed of course and won't open until Thursday. According to the computer system, the order was still in process. I'm hoping they ship it out Thursday, which means I should get it Friday."

"Fingers crossed," she said. "Taking this group to work is going to be tricky, but I need to open the store on Thursday."

"Maybe we could talk Jillian into staying with them for part of the day." He took his cutter to the sink.

She nodded. "That's a good idea. I could take Archie with the four that are used to going to the store, and that would leave her with the five smaller ones. If I'm not busy, I can close early, but I need to make up what I lost in sales on those days before Christmas."

He nodded. "Depending on how busy I am, I can adjust my schedule too. I'll cover paying Jillian to come over. It's my fault you're in this mess with the dogs."

She shook her head. "It's not your fault. I said yes." She

walked to the fridge. "I think you can start the grill and get those steaks on. The ravioli will only take a few minutes. I don't think we'll need potatoes, do you?"

The doorbell ringing and then the cacophony of barking and whining that ensued interrupted them.

"Who could that be?" she asked, wiping her hands on a towel and heading toward the front door.

She looked through the glass and saw the smiling faces of Rusty and Mabel poking out of their hooded jackets. Gina smiled and opened the door wide. "Merry Christmas, you two. What are you doing out and about?"

Rusty held out two pink boxes to her. "Fresh from the oven. We've been down at the café trying to get some of the orders out."

Mabel giggled. "Just for our favorite customers. Without power, we couldn't get them all done, of course. We decided to call it a day."

Gina motioned them inside. "Come on in."

"Oh, we don't want to interrupt you," said Rusty.

"Nonsense. You two are on your own this year, right?"

Mabel nodded. "Yep, and with this crazy storm, it's a good thing we weren't expecting the kids home."

"Why don't you join us for Christmas Eve dinner? We're just getting it started."

Rusty frowned. "We? I thought you were on your own. I remember you said that when you ordered the pies."

Gina shrugged and rolled her eyes. "Well, that was the plan, but Tommy Lane is here staying with me." She motioned them inside, both of their brows raised, giving her a quizzical look.

She took the pie boxes and added, "Come in and I'll explain. It's not as risqué as it sounds.

CHAPTER 11

Christmas morning, Gina woke in her own comfy bed, having spent Christmas Eve sharing the steak and ravioli dinner she and Tommy had planned with Rusty and Mabel. They topped it off with slices of Mabel's delicious pies and tons of laughter and visiting until almost midnight.

The couple played with the dogs, and Mabel held Pixie most of the night. Gina tried to talk her into adopting, but with all the time they spent at the café, they wouldn't be able to give her the attention she craved.

After sending them home with some ravioli, Gina insisted Tommy sleep in Luke's bed instead of spending another night on the couch. She helped him attach the wire panels together to make a freestanding pen for the bedroom, like they had used on the porch. Once his bedroom floor was protected, they carried all the shelter dogs and put them in it, along with Archie, who seemed to calm the smaller ones. She let her dogs, along with Hank and Finn, sleep in her bedroom, albeit on the floor.

Waking up without a sore back or a kink in her neck was

glorious. She stretched and added her warm cardigan to her pajamas, the pants covered in skiing sheep instead of penguins. The dogs followed her into the living room where the Christmas tree glowed.

Without the fire being their only source of heat, they hadn't worried about getting up to feed it, and now only embers were left. She used the poker to separate them, added some newspaper and kindling, plus a few puffs of air, and was rewarded with new flames. She waited for the kindling to burn hot and added a log.

Once the fire roared, she added more logs and wandered into the kitchen, lured by the aroma of fresh coffee. If she were a cat, she would be purring. She loved electricity and all the convenience it delivered.

After pouring a cup, she made breakfast for the dogs, lining up bowls on the counter. Her kitchen was spotless, thanks to everyone pitching in last night, washing and drying dishes and cleaning all the surfaces.

She had put together a breakfast treat, Luke's favorite, made from frozen rolls, cinnamon and sugar, lots of butter, and pecans. She made two of them, so she could share with Virginia and the girls. They were in pans on the counter and had risen overnight. The dough was puffed high and ready to slide into the oven.

She turned it on to preheat while she fed the four dogs who were focused on their bowls. As they ate, she stepped onto the back porch and looked outside. Sunshine and blue skies framed the snow-covered valley, promising a beautiful day.

She let the dogs into the yard and slipped breakfast into the oven before sliding onto one of the stools at the counter to savor her coffee. Several minutes later, Otis tapped on the porch door, like he did most mornings, signaling he was ready to come back inside. She gathered towels, fresh from the laundry she had finished last night, and proceeded to wipe all their paws.

With that done, they scurried into the living room, settling into their beds near the fireplace.

Moments later, the door of Luke's bedroom clicked, and Tommy came into the kitchen, freshly showered and smiling. "I smell something sugary." He sniffed in the air. "And coffee."

"Help yourself. I'm baking a breakfast treat that will be ready in a few minutes. I made one for Virginia, too."

"I'll take Archie and the littles outside and then come back for coffee. Then we can set up the enclosure for them in the living room."

"How did they do last night?"

"I never heard a peep from any of them. I think they were worn out from all the activity yesterday and not getting to bed until late."

She helped him transfer the dogs from the bedroom to the porch, and then she folded the panels down and carried them into the living room.

The buzzer on the oven sounded, so she hurried to take the bread out and placed both pans on the stovetop to cool. The sugar and cinnamon had melted together, oozing sweetness throughout the dough. She couldn't wait to sample it.

Remembering the dogs would be back soon, she rushed back to her task and set up the fencing diagonally between the two walls. Hank was very curious and kept sticking his nose on her hand as she manipulated the panels. While she was there, she added a log to the fire.

She had time to turn the warm pans over and place the mound of rolls infused with caramelized sugar and browned to perfection, on serving platters. When Tommy returned with the shelter dogs, she traded him one platter and asked him to deliver it next door while she tackled the drying of the dogs.

Tommy had kept them confined to a small area, so their sweaters remained dry, and she only had to dry their paws and get them fed before transporting them to the living room to settle into their blankets and beds with the other dogs. Archie had proven himself to be trustworthy, and she left him outside the fencing with the other dogs.

Part of her wanted to leave them all out of the pen, but she didn't quite trust Pudge, Pixie, or Olive and knew if they were left alone, they would just bark, so Gonzo and Stubbs would have to suffer with them.

By the time she had them settled, Tommy was in the kitchen, pouring coffee. She sliced off two generous pieces of the sweet bread and slid them into place in front of the stools at the counter before adding more coffee to her cup.

She took her first bite and closed her eyes. It tasted like Christmas. Like family.

Tommy raved about it and helped himself to a second slice. "This is addictive. So good."

"It's a Christmas morning tradition in our family, and I'm so glad I was able to bake it today. It's Luke's favorite treat."

He ran the last bite across his plate, picking up all the stray pecan bits, and popped it in his mouth. "I can see why."

She grinned. "Don't fill up on it, I have another surprise for you." She slid off the stool and went to the small counter at the far end of the kitchen, where behind a stack of cookbooks, she unearthed a glass cake plate.

She carried it and a small, wrapped package to the island counter and placed them in front of Tommy. "I tried to think of something equally impressive as getting those Christmas lights going for me. Merry Christmas, Tommy."

His eyes widened as he took in the layer cake covered in thick, coconut-pecan frosting. "I can't believe you made this for me. It looks delicious."

"Well, I knew I couldn't go shopping and wanted you to

have something special this Christmas. It hasn't been a traditional one for sure but having you here has made it so much better. I couldn't have managed without your help."

His eyes didn't move from the cake. "This is really special. The lights were no big deal. All I did was plug them into that little emergency power box I keep in my truck." He sighed. "This, this took some real work."

He turned his eyes that matched the color of the sky to her. "I can't tell you what this means to me." He smiled. "I also can't wait to dig into it."

"It's our dessert for tonight. I'm going to bake a ham, make some potatoes, a grape salad, and of course ravioli."

"That all sounds perfect. I won't even tell you what I would have been eating had I stayed at my place for Christmas. Being here, with you, has made it the best one I've had in a long time."

She pointed at the small, wrapped box next to the cake. "Open it."

He shook his head. "The cake is more than enough." She noticed the twinkle in his eye as he tore into the package.

He held up a ticket to the New Year's Eve party at Cedar Mountain Lodge and looked at her with confusion.

She pointed at the ticket. "I'm going with Luke and Jo, and he picked me up an extra ticket in case I wanted to bring a friend... or a plus one... or whatever. I thought after all you've been through, it might be fun."

"I've always heard about the party, but I've never been." He gritted his teeth. "I'm not sure I have anything to wear. I'm not much of a dress-up guy."

She thought about the black dress she had purchased for the party. She was looking forward to glamming it up and dressing fancy, since all she ever wore were jeans and sweaters. It wasn't a black-tie-required kind of event. The lodge mixed it up each year and this year, it was an anything-goes kind of evening. They were featuring a country band with line dancing.

She shoved aside her desire to wear the glamorous dress. "I'm not dressing up. It's not required, and they've got a country band this year. I hope you'll come. It's always tons of fun." She wiggled her brows. "Not to mention great food, and I do recall you saying you never pass up a free meal."

"You're a tough negotiator." He flicked the ticket between his fingers. "Okay, you've got a date."

He fumbled the ticket, and it dropped to the floor. "I mean not exactly a date, uh… sorry, I'm a little rusty at this."

He bent to pick up the ticket at the same time she did, and they bumped their heads together. "Oww," she said, grabbing the top of her head. "Sorry."

He picked up the ticket. "My fault."

"I haven't been on a date in years." She laughed. "I don't want to make you nervous or uncomfortable, so let's just go together as friends. Does that sound okay?"

The redness on his cheeks blossomed as he nodded. "That would be perfect." He glanced at the calendar on the refrigerator. "I usually work that day, but I'll make sure I'm off in plenty of time. I can pick you up around six if that works."

She took a swallow from her cup. "Oh, I can just meet you there. I don't want you to go to any trouble."

He shook his head. "I may not have had a dad growing up, but your dad taught me and my brothers how to be gentleman. He would slap me silly if I let a lady drive herself."

She could picture her dad teaching the fatherless boys how to behave like gentleman. "You're right. That wouldn't go over well with Dad at all. I'll be ready. Mom and Dad are taking charge of Ollie and Grace and all four dogs that night."

"At least we won't have to worry about the guest dogs by then. That would be too much for your mom and dad."

She nodded. "Jo and Luke always celebrate and stay up at the lodge for a couple of nights, since he proposed to Jo at the New Year's Eve event. I think it's sweet and romantic. Last year, Maddie stayed with the kids, but this year, Mom and Dad offered."

"Jo and Luke are perfect for each other. They're a great match and both such good people."

She cleared away the breakfast dishes. "I think so, too. Jo is like having another sister. She's great for Luke. They've had some struggles with the kids but have settled into a routine, and they're both so good with them."

"I'm just glad those two kids have a shot at a great future."

❆

Gina spent the rest of the morning getting things prepped for Christmas dinner, while Tommy watched some television and minded the dogs. He took them out in the yard several times and let the snow-loving dogs play and romp together. Gonzo even got in on the fun and took a liking to the snow, but the others preferred to stay indoors near the fire.

In the early afternoon, with the sun shining and making it feel warmer than it was, Tommy suggested they take the dogs for a walk around the neighborhood. Sick of being stuck inside for too many days on end, Gina was eager to agree.

It took some time to get all of them organized, but they were soon out the front door and walking along the now-cleared sidewalks. The air was crisp, but the sun warmed them and glistened off the fresh snow, making it look as if someone had sprinkled glitter on everything, or they were inside one of the cute little snow globes.

It was spectacular and made Gina think of what her girls were missing by spending Christmas break in sunny Florida. Snow and cold weather could be annoying, as was the lack of power the past few days, but she couldn't imagine Christmas without the white stuff and the view of the mountains that never failed to stun her.

As they made their way back to the house, Tommy's cell phone rang. They had to stop, and she took hold of the leashes while he pulled off his glove to answer.

After a short conversation, he disconnected. "I've got a customer with a little problem. I need to run over and see if I can get them going, or their Christmas dinner will be ruined."

He took hold of the leashes, and Gina led them home. As they ushered the dogs onto the back porch, he bent down to get a towel. "Sorry to leave you with them, but I shouldn't be long."

She shook her head as she dried Pudge. "Not a problem. I'm just going to get dinner in the oven and watch a Christmas movie." She gestured to the dogs waiting to be dried. "They should be tired after all the activity. Maybe we can all squeeze in a nap before dinner."

"Okay, I'll be as quick as I can." He made sure the door latched behind him.

After she had dried all the dogs and got them settled in the living room, she put together the cheesy potato dish and got the ham in the oven.

She put in a video call to Raylynn and Megan, but they didn't answer. Minutes later, her phone pinged with a text from Megan, letting her know they were eating but would call her later.

She made herself a cup of tea and settled into her recliner to watch one of her favorite seasonal movies about a man in the military who visits a little town in hopes of finding the woman who sent him a Christmas card.

As she watched it, her mind drifted to Tommy. There weren't too many guys like him who would do a house call on Christmas. Or business owners who worked the holidays so his crew could spend time with their families. Or who donated so much of his time and money to a good cause like Love Links.

There was something holding him back from a fuller life, though. Growing up as he had, it was understandable that he'd be reluctant to have a family. She remembered him saying he felt like he'd already done that.

He deserved more.

Even if he didn't think so.

CHAPTER 12

When Gina got up the day after Christmas, she gazed at the black dress hanging from her closet door and the strappy heels on the floor below it. She'd have to wait for another occasion to wear the ensemble and think of something else a bit more casual.

By the time she wandered out to the kitchen for her first cup of coffee, Tommy had already left for the day. He wanted to get an early start and knock off early, hoping to be back by three o'clock, so Gina wouldn't have to close her shop early. Gina had talked to Jillian, and she was more than willing to sit with the shelter dogs as long as was needed.

She glanced at her phone, checking to see if she had missed the girls calling, but there was nothing since the text from last night. Her heart ached, thinking about her future. She hated the idea of being relegated to waiting by her phone to hear from her daughters, who obviously weren't thinking about her. She didn't want to be that sad mom, desperate to be a part of their lives.

Hopefully, the excitement of Don's new place and the beach would wear off.

Right.

Who was she kidding?

After getting ready for the day, she fed the pack of dogs and gobbled down a piece of the leftover cinnamon bread with her coffee. As she swallowed the last bite, the front door bell rang.

Gina welcomed Jillian inside and showed her the ropes. She elected to leave Archie with them, since he seemed to calm the others. She made sure Jillian knew how to leash the dogs and then helped her take them out into the backyard. "Don't let them go off the leash and only bring them out here. They're a handful, and you don't need any drama."

Jillian laughed as she wrangled them in the snow, trying to keep them from getting too wet. After showing her around the kitchen and telling her to help herself to food or snacks, Gina added a couple of logs to the fire, making sure Jillian was comfortable with the process.

With the dogs inside their corral in the living room, Gina slipped into her coat and boots and led her four charges out the front door and around to the garage. Their tails wagged as they waited to jump into the backseat.

Once at the store, Gina went about her normal duties and restocked the small freezer in the front of the store. She organized all her Christmas-themed pet accessories and made a sign advertising them at fifty percent off. She added some sale stickers in her front window, hoping to draw in some bargain hunters.

She opted for lunch at Fox and Hound between waiting on a few of her regular customers, plus meeting the new pet parents of several of the adoptees from last weekend. The problem at the shelter had forced Gabby to place the dogs without being able to do her usual due diligence, so dog placements were temporary, but that didn't stop the new owners from stocking up on supplies for their new family members.

She got rid of a few Christmassy toys and sold several bags of food. The power outage had prompted people to be more prepared and have a backup supply of pet food. While ringing up a sale, her phone pinged with a text.

As soon as she helped the last customer, she checked her phone. Tommy had sent a message letting her know the part for the shelter had shipped out, and it would be delivered tomorrow afternoon.

As much as she enjoyed the dogs, it was tough to manage her responsibilities and them. Thank goodness the girls were staying with Virginia. When she had chatted with her neighbor on the phone, it was clear the arrangement was working, and Virginia sounded quite happy.

In the mid-afternoon, Leslie texted to confirm dinner plans and their meeting at the lodge. Part of her wanted to cancel. The timing was less than ideal, but Gina remembered what it was like moving back home and longing for a connection outside of her family. She tapped in a response, using lots of happy emojis, and promised to meet her there.

Business had waned in the last hour, and Gina turned off her open sign thirty minutes earlier than usual. She rounded up the dogs and headed home, hoping Tommy was home by now.

She spotted his truck in the driveway and sighed. "You boys need to be good for Tommy tonight while I'm gone."

Otis and Watson looked at her with serious faces, as if they could understand every word.

She hustled them through the front door and walked in to find Tommy just coming from her bedroom.

She frowned, and he held up his hands.

"Olive is missing. I've looked everywhere else. I was just

looking in there in case she somehow managed to sneak in your room. I told Jillian to go home, as I know Olive's in the house somewhere, but I haven't been able to find her. Jillian said she'd be back tomorrow morning."

Gina set her purse down in the kitchen and helped him search every corner of the house again. She even checked the basket on the front porch, thinking maybe Olive picked up a tip from Pixie.

Tommy huffed. "I've scoured the living room and kitchen. Jillian had the gate down between the kitchen and living room, since she was going back and forth, so that would have been the escape route."

Gina laughed. "Oh, these little dogs are sneaky. I'm glad I have big ones that I can easily see if they try to hide." While Tommy turned his attention to the back porch, she looked under the Christmas tree with a flashlight, thinking they might have missed Olive's dark coat in the cover of the branches.

No luck.

She sat on the floor in front of the tree. "Where would I go if I were Olive?" She noticed Otis, Winston, and Finn surrounding her recliner, all of them with their noses sniffing at the back of it.

They were onto something.

Hopefully, one naughty little long-haired Chihuahua.

Gina lifted the skirting along the bottom of the chair and shined the flashlight under it, placing her head on the floor to see. She caught the glint of an eyeball and shook her head.

"Tommy, we found her," she hollered.

He came rushing into the room and took great care to move the chair while Gina kept her head on the floor to guide him. With the chair high enough, she reached in and extracted the little rascal.

Olive, unaware of all the trouble she had caused, looked no worse for wear. Tommy set the chair down and took the dog from Gina, stroking her as he walked her to the enclosure and put her with the other dogs.

He pointed at the wire panels and shook his head. "Obviously, it's too easy for the little ones to escape between the panel and the wall. I think we'll have to connect the panels into a circle again. It means less space, but I'm about over the hide and seek game."

"I agree, and we can keep Archie and Gonzo out with the big dogs. They're both behaving and tend to stick close to the others. That will make more room for the smaller dogs."

He took the end of the wire panel and herded the dogs to the other side while he connected it to the other end. "Gonzo is a great dog. I've been thinking about asking Paul to consider adopting him for Davey. I think a dog would be great for him."

Gina's smile widened. "Oh, that's a great idea. He's a real love and deserves a boy in his life."

She gave each of the dogs who had helped them find Olive a treat and a thorough belly rub before popping into the kitchen to get all the dogs' dinners prepared. With the bowls set on the counter, she put a sticky note next to each of them so Tommy would know which bowl went to each of the dogs.

"I've got to get changed and get a move on to meet Leslie," she said, passing through the living room on her way to her bedroom. "I've got their dinners ready, and I won't be too late."

"Don't rush on my account. I have big plans for leftovers and a marathon of a car show I enjoy watching."

"You sound like my dad. He loves those shows."

She changed into a pair of clean jeans and a cranberry-colored sweater her mom had given her last year. It reminded her of Christmas and was warm. She added a pair of wine-colored ankle boots and some earrings before dashing to the door.

As she slipped into her jacket, Tommy glanced over at her. "Enjoy your dinner and don't rush home. We'll be fine."

She smiled and wrapped a scarf around her neck. "I will, thanks. If you need anything, just call my cell."

She opened the door, and he called out, "Oh, and Gina…"

"Yeah," she said, meeting his eyes.

"You look nice."

The scarf was suddenly too hot as the heat rose from her neck to her face. After several seconds, she untied her tongue and said, "Thank you. I'll see you soon." She closed the door, anxious to let the cold air cool her face.

She'd never been flustered around Tommy before.

Something had changed over these last few days.

❆

It was after ten o'clock when Gina parked her truck in the garage and made her way to the front door. She opened it quietly, hoping not to disturb the dogs and set off a chorus of barking.

Tommy was in the recliner, his feet up, the television tuned to one of his car shows. The only light in the room came from the television and the glow of the lights on the tree. All four dogs plus Gonzo and Archie surrounded Tommy's chair, sleeping, while Zap was sprawled across Tommy's lap. Otis, Watson, and Finn noticed her and raised their heads, but the others didn't stir. Zap opened her eye and looked at her but snuggled closer to Tommy's chest and remained quiet.

Gina took off her boots and coat and tiptoed across the floor. When she got closer to the chair, she could see Tommy had fallen asleep. She elected to let him sleep, transferring Gonzo and Archie into the enclosure for the rest of the night.

She herded the other four dogs to her bedroom, changed into her pajamas, and fell into bed. She had enjoyed visiting with Leslie, and the meal was superb, but she was exhausted.

Leslie, who had always been talkative and outgoing, dominated the evening with her nonstop conversation. In a way, it had been nice, since all Gina had to do was nod and agree with her periodically.

Leslie had been working around the clock at the tree farm and was ready for a break before she started her upgrades. With her dad passing away and her mom unable to do much, she had taken the reins and was intent on making the farm a destination for events and weddings, along with expanding the offerings and wanted to grow pumpkins and put in a corn maze for the fall holidays.

She even considered growing flowers. Leslie also told her the family dog, a sweet Labrador, had passed away shortly after her dad. She and her mom hoped to find another dog, since he had been such good company. Gina let her know about Archie, who she thought would be a perfect choice to be a great companion and would enjoy running through the acres of trees at the farm.

As Gina rested her head on her pillow, she realized part of her exhaustion came from listening to Leslie talk about all her projects. At the same time she touted her plans, Leslie told Gina she hoped to avoid seeing Eric much.

As she rambled on, it was clear they hadn't mended their fences. Gina could relate since interacting with Don was not her favorite activity, but she also didn't move to where he lived.

Leslie had inquired if Gina was seeing anyone but barely took a breath and didn't give her time to answer. She wasn't sure how to answer that question. A week ago, she would have said no. Now, she wasn't so sure.

CHAPTER 13

❄

Tommy ended up staying over Friday night, after working to get the shelter up and running. By the time he finished, he was the only one in the building, and it was too late to transfer the dogs.

Tommy promised Gabby he'd transport them to the shelter on Saturday morning. Well, all except for Gonzo since Paul had agreed to adopt him. Davey's birthday party was the first Saturday in January, and Tommy would keep Gonzo at his house until then, when he planned to surprise Davey with the best birthday gift ever.

Gina's phone woke her before five o'clock with a call from Raylynn and Megan. They had forgotten about the time change and apologized for forgetting to call her on Christmas. They were just so busy, and time had slipped away from them.

Despite being disoriented and half-asleep, she loved hearing their voices and was happy they were enjoying their time with Don. They chattered nonstop about going out in his boat, the fancy restaurants they had enjoyed, and all the time they spent at the beach. She didn't have time to tell them anything about the shelter dogs or the storm before they rushed to say goodbye, as they were on their way to breakfast and a shopping excursion.

Gina stayed in bed, trying to go back to sleep, but only managed to do so thirty minutes before she had to get up and get ready for work.

After enjoying a cup of coffee and splurging on a piece of German chocolate cake with Tommy, Gina set out for the shop on Saturday morning, leaving Tommy in charge of the zoo. Gina unloaded her dogs, along with Finn and Hank, and went about her morning routine at Wags and Whiskers. As soon as she got the store opened, Gina put in a call to Gabby at the shelter.

Gabby had a wonderful way of matching animals with people and while she wasn't pushy, she'd been known to go out of her way to take potential adoptees on several home visits. She reminded Gina of Mr. Lott, who had been her dad's friend and a car salesman. Mr. Lott used to deliver new cars to the homes of anybody who showed the slightest interest. He'd let them drive it around for a few days to see if they liked it. It worked like a charm. Her dad always said he was the best salesman ever and sold more cars that way.

Gina let her know Leslie was interested in Archie. She also dropped Virginia's name as a possible match for Pixie. Once Virginia was fully healed and able to get around better, Gina thought Pixie would make a great companion for her, and Virginia could provide a warm lap for Pixie. Gabby was thrilled and promised to do all she could to make an adoption happen for Archie and Pixie.

Gina laughed as she ended the conversation with Gabby, telling her she was impressed that she and Tommy had a potential adoption rate of fifty percent of the dogs they had sheltered. Gabby had some leads on the other three and hoped to get them placed in homes during the first week of January.

Gina's heart warmed at the idea of all the dogs getting their forever families. As much of a hassle as it had been, it had been worth it to keep the dogs safe. Not to mention, she'd gotten to know Tommy on a more personal level.

Like the sweet dogs, he hadn't had the easiest life and could use a forever family. It would be hard to say goodbye to him.

She didn't have time to dwell on her impending sadness. Saturdays were generally busy, and this one was no exception. Main Street bustled with shoppers and by the time she closed the store, Gina was tired. She was ready for a quiet evening and a good night's sleep.

Tomorrow, she had to drive to Boise and retrieve her family from the airport. She couldn't wait to see all of them.

Her cheerful Christmas lights greeted her as she drove down the street and parked in the breezeway. Tommy's truck was no longer in the driveway. At the sight of the empty space, her spirits wavered.

She let the dogs out to run in the yard and made her way inside. The house was quiet. She filled the kettle with water and turned it on, ready for a cup of tea and whatever leftovers she could put together.

She noticed Tommy had restored order to her back porch and even put away the storage bins and wire enclosure. The safety gates were all stacked in a neat pile, and her living room furniture had been returned to normal. Everything was shipshape, with the tree lights glowing and a fire burning in the hearth.

She found a note on the granite-topped island from Tommy. GOT EVERYTHING CLEANED UP, I HOPE. I WASHED THE BLANKETS AND SHEETS WE USED FOR THE DOGS AND LEFT THEM FOLDED ON THE TABLE. MY SHEETS ARE CLEAN. THANKS FOR letting me stay. I'll see you on New Year's Eve. Call me if you need anything—Tommy (Zap and Gonzo too). p.s. I left you a piece of cake and will return your platter soon.

She smiled as she read the note again, happy that Gonzo would be with Tommy. She fed the dogs, and they settled on their beds in front of the fire.

She opened the fridge, looking for something that sounded good. Finally, she dished out some potatoes to reheat in the microwave and added a bit of honey to her tea before taking her dinner into the living room. She topped it off with the piece of cake Tommy had thoughtfully left for her.

She watched television while she ate, willing herself to focus on the program and not on the overwhelming silence in her house. She caught herself turning to talk to Tommy, the smile fading from her face when she remembered he wasn't there.

After trying and failing to concentrate on the episode she was watching, she turned off the television and padded to her bedroom. Excited to see her family tomorrow and willing her mind to focus on that, she crawled under the covers, relenting and letting all four dogs crawl on top of her bed.

She didn't have the energy to make them stay on the floor and was too lonely to care.

❄

Sunday morning, she booted the dogs off her bed and let them loose in the backyard. As much as she missed the other dogs, it was nice to be able to let them go out on their own and not worry about them.

She wandered into the living room with a cup of coffee.

Tommy had even put the Christmas gifts back under the tree. Tonight at Luke's, there'd be pizza and pie. She smiled thinking about getting to see Ollie and Grace open their gifts and hear everything about her family's trip to California.

Otis and Watson would miss having Hank and Finn around. After tonight, her house would return to a sense of normal. Normal was going to be very quiet compared to the last few days. Thank goodness for her two dogs or she'd never survive having her girls out of the house.

She heard the dogs at the back door and brought them inside, dried them off, and gave them breakfast. She poured another cup of coffee and went into the living room.

As if they knew she was struggling, Otis and Watson moved closer to her, Otis with his head in her lap and Watson crawling up to snuggle with her on the couch. The sting of tears burned in her throat. She swallowed another gulp of coffee.

She wasn't usually so emotional, but the holidays were always a little tougher than other times. Her mind wandered to the early years with her girls at Christmas; knowing she'd never get those days back left her longing for the past.

She forced herself away from those memories and what she thought she'd lost, to being able to see her parents, Luke, and his family and celebrate Christmas with them.

Her girls would be home in less than a week and then things would be better. At least until summer, when they'd be gone again. With Raylynn going to Florida in the fall, Gina was worried Megan would want to transfer there and live with Don while she finished her last two years of high school. She could almost feel it coming.

If she were right, the two years she thought she had would dwindle to just a few months. She told herself she'd be strong and wouldn't hold Megan back if that's what she wanted to do. Don was a good father, and Gina's fears of living alone weren't a reason to deny her daughter the opportunity to spend time with Don and be closer to Raylynn if that's what she wanted to do. Megan hadn't said anything, but the idea had been nagging at Gina since Raylynn made the decision to go to college there.

She checked the time, surprised that she had been sitting there for so long and after washing her cup, she went to get ready for her trip to Boise.

❄

Their plane was on time and just after one o'clock, Luke slid behind the wheel of Jo's SUV. Jo was in the back section of seats with Ollie and Grace, and Gina and her mom sat in the middle, with Ray taking the passenger seat.

The whole way home, Gina twisted in her seat so she could chat with the kids and tell them all about her adventures with the shelter dogs. They were so excited and kept laughing when she talked about Pixie hiding from them and then losing Olive.

When they got to town, Luke dropped his mom and dad at their house. They waved goodbye with a promise to see everyone at Luke's for dinner.

Jo crawled into the middle section of seats for the short trip to the house. She gripped Gina's arm. "So, Tommy spent all that time at your house? I want to hear all about it."

Gina shrugged. "It was nice. He's nice."

Jo grinned and gripped her arm tighter. "I knew it. That little sparkle in your eye tells me all I need to know." She hollered up to Luke. "Did you hear that? Tommy and Gina got stuck spending Christmas together. He stayed at her house almost this whole time."

Luke chuckled as he turned onto their street. "Tommy's a good guy. More than good, he's one of the best."

Gina blushed. "I invited him to come to the New Year's Eve party up at the lodge."

Jo bounced in her seat. "That's terrific. I'm so glad he said yes."

Luke pulled into the driveway and shut off the ignition. "You must have quite the effect on him. Tommy isn't one to socialize much. We've included him in lots of invitations, but he's always working. He must like you." He wiggled his brows at his sister as he removed their luggage from the cargo area.

Gina shrugged. "I enjoyed having him around. He's easy to be with." She slipped out the door and helped Jo unbuckle the kids. "Oh, he seemed a little worried about not having the right clothes, so I decided to go casual instead of the fancy dress we discussed."

Jo shook her head. "Aww, that's so sweet. Luke and I haven't been anywhere that warrants dressing up since last year, so we're going all out, but there will be a good mix, so don't let that worry you."

The kids couldn't wait to get inside and see their dogs. Gina had left Hank and Finn at the house, knowing how anxious Ollie and Grace would be to see them.

Jo led the kids inside while Gina helped Luke carry all their luggage.

By the time they got to the door, the kids were rolling on the floor, squealing with the dogs licking them and snuggling with them. It warmed Gina's heart to see them so happy and full of laughter.

Gina set down the bags she was carrying and looked at her brother. "Your generator worked like a charm, and we checked on the house a couple of times. Everything seemed fine, and Tommy even shoveled your walkways."

Luke grinned. "I told you he was a good guy. A keeper if I ever saw one." He moved closer to Gina and hugged her.

"Thanks for taking care of everything. I know it was a hassle with the power outage."

"I'll pick up the pies from Mabel and be back tonight. See you then." She hugged him again, thankful he was home. Having him and Jo along with her parents around always helped Gina feel stronger. "I sure missed you guys."

Luke walked her to the door. "We're going to get these two down for a nap so they're not a handful tonight. See you in a few hours. Thanks again."

Gina waved goodbye and hopped in her truck. His mention of a nap sounded like a good idea, but first, she drove downtown to pick up the pies.

CHAPTER 14

❄

New Year's Eve, like most of the stores along Main Street, Gina closed at two o'clock. That gave her time to stop by the market on the way home. She picked up a few things, along with Virginia's order, which she delivered as soon as she got home.

Virginia looked much better, and the girls had the house gleaming. True to her word, Virginia had convinced Megan to attend the community college, and she would be starting classes in mid-January.

Along with suggesting Leslie adopt Archie, Gina had also let her know that Jillian was interested in horticulture and loved the outdoors. With her expansion, Leslie needed more help and liked the idea of a young woman eager to learn. She extended an invitation to Jillian to come out to the farm in late January and see if they were a good fit.

By then, Virginia should be on the road to recovery and able to do more. She invited the girls to stay as long as they had jobs or were going to school. She wouldn't charge them any rent and in exchange, they would help her with chores and errands.

Despite all the hardships of the storm, things had worked out and in addition to helping some dogs find new homes, Gina's spirits lifted at the news of the girls becoming a more permanent part of the neighborhood.

She left them all with hugs and good wishes before getting back to her house and the dogs. She curled into the couch with a cup of hot tea, intent on watching more of her show and hoping to catch a little nap before Tommy arrived.

❄

She woke over an hour later, surprised she had slept so long but felt refreshed and confident she could stay up until midnight.

She got the dogs fed and let them out while she picked out an outfit, finally settling on dark jeans and a blue sweater that matched her eyes, topped with a faux-suede jacket and boots.

She was scrolling through her emails and checking social media when the dogs sprang from their beds and rushed to the front door. She checked the time. Tommy was early.

She went to the front door and opened it to find Tommy standing on the porch. She did a double-take.

Gina sucked in a breath.

He was wearing a dark-blue suit with a crisp-white shirt and deep-blue tie. Her mouth hung open as she took in all his handsomeness.

He grinned, and her stomach fluttered.

"What are you doing? I thought you didn't have a suit."

He shrugged. "After I saw that black dress hanging on your closet, I knew I couldn't let it go to waste. I made a trip to Boise, and Mike's wife took me shopping."

She reached for his hand. "Come in. Come in. I'll go get changed."

He moved his hand from behind his back and handed her a bouquet of red roses. "For you."

Tears stung her eyes. "Oh, my, they're gorgeous. Thank you." She took them and ushered him into the house.

As she hurried to the kitchen to put the flowers in water, she said, "Just give me a few minutes, and I'll be ready."

He was on the couch, already petting Otis and Watson, talking to them in a soft voice.

She took the hallway from the kitchen to her bedroom, flinging off her clothes, pulling on her black nylons, and slipping into the black beaded dress. She added sparkling earrings and the strappy shoes.

After checking herself from every angle and another trip to the bathroom to make sure her hair was okay, she returned to the living room.

At the sound of her footsteps, Tommy and the dogs turned their attention toward her. "Wowza, you look beautiful."

He pushed the dogs from the couch and stood, staring at her.

"Thank you. I've been excited to wear it and dress up, since I rarely do."

"Well, you're stunning. I'm glad I saw it and bought the suit." He grinned.

"I guess we owe Olive for leading you on that wild goose chase through the house."

He bent his head toward the door. "Are you ready to head up to the lodge?"

She nodded. "I just need to find my wrap. My other outfit was lots warmer." She rifled through the closet and removed a black wrap trimmed in faux fur.

Tommy held it for her and placed it around her shoulders. He offered her his arm. "Shall we?"

She gave him her ticket to hold for her and made sure he

still had the key she had given him to her house. She didn't have pockets and didn't want to keep track of it.

They walked to his truck, and he held the door for her as she climbed into the passenger seat. With the roads dried and clear weather, it didn't take long to make the drive up the mountain.

As always, Cedar Mountain Lodge was decked out in her holiday best. Lights twinkled from every bush, and the huge tree strung with thousands of lights caught Gina's eye. It was the perfect holiday setting and no matter how many times she visited, she was awestruck.

Tommy eased the truck under the portico, and a valet greeted them. Tommy took Gina's arm as they walked up the steps to the main entrance of the lodge. She pointed to the left. "The party's not in the main building."

He nodded. "I know, but I haven't been here yet this year to see the tree, and I know how much you love trees."

The fresh scent of pine greeted them as Tommy opened the huge wooden door. Soft piano music filled the air, and the lobby bustled with guests on their way to the big event.

Tommy led her toward the roaring fireplace and the magnificent tree that graced the lobby. Hundreds of red ornaments glinted among its branches. It was stunning.

After they admired it for a few minutes, he took her hand and walked across the lobby to the doors at the back of the lodge. "The view out here is one of my favorites."

She agreed and followed him along the spotless walkways, taking in the snow-covered trees and bushes along the way. He stopped at the little bridge and gazed up at the dark mountains. The moonlight glinted off the snow while the song the band was playing drifted through the air.

The stillness and the beauty were nothing short of magical.

He took her hand in his. "I'm more than a little rusty at

anything resembling dating, but I... well, I wanted to ask if it would be okay if we spent more time together. Maybe went to dinner or the movies or whatever you like to do." He took a quick breath and continued, "This last week... spending it with you and the crazy bunch of dogs has been the best week of my life. I don't think I realized what I was missing. I've sort of resolved myself to a lonely life, substituting work for anything resembling a relationship. I don't want to live like that anymore."

Tears glistened in Gina's eyes as she smiled at him. "I feel the same way about you. These last couple of days with you gone, I've been miserable. After my marriage failed, like you, I accepted the fact that I'd be on my own and channeled all my energy into the girls. Now, the realization that they'll be gone soon, has really hit me. I don't want this to be the end for me either."

He bent closer to her, and she tilted her head towards him. Their lips met and sent a spark of electricity through Gina, making her arms and legs tingle. Tommy wrapped his arms around her and instead of pulling away, he deepened the kiss.

All thoughts flew out of Gina's head as she relished the warmth and connection his touch brought to her. He finally pulled his lips from hers and bent to touch his forehead against hers. "I've been dreaming of doing that since that first night at your house."

She laughed, a huge belly laugh, and kissed him again. "Me, too."

He took her hands in his. "I guess we better get to the party. Luke and Jo will be wondering where we are."

She leaned against his shoulder and gazed back toward the lodge, the glow of the lights against the snow creating a gorgeous backdrop. "Just one more minute. I don't want to forget this perfect moment."

He slipped his arm around hers as they took in the view.

A couple walked by them on their way to the party, and Gina looked up at Tommy. "I guess we better get a move on. Jo and Luke are going to be beyond excited when we tell them the news."

"Maybe we can keep it sort of quiet until later. Just going to this party is a huge step for me, and I don't think I can deal with that kind of attention tonight."

They walked toward the building, and she nodded. "I understand. It can be our secret for tonight."

He smiled and squeezed her shoulder a little tighter.

As they walked, he asked, "Are you up for a little road trip Saturday? I'd like to introduce you to my family at Davey's birthday party."

"I'd love that. I can't wait to see how he reacts to Gonzo. You'll be his favorite uncle forever."

He chuckled. "That's my plan."

She reached for his hand. "By the way, you can hold onto that key to my house."

He laughed and brought her hand to his chest. "I'd offer you one, but you already have the key to my heart."

She leaned closer as they reached the door, ready to face the new year and whatever it brought, together.

EPILOGUE

Davey loved his gift and he and Gonzo are best friends. More than anything this series is about family. With that in mind, Luke's big sister was a character we met in CHRISTMAS WISHES, and Gina has been begging for her own story ever since. With Luke and Jo settled and the addition of Grace and Ollie to their family, this was the perfect time for readers to get to know more about Gina. Tommy was introduced in CHRISTMAS SURPRISES and Jo thought he'd be the perfect guy for her much-loved sister-in-law. Turns out, she was onto something.

Both Gina and Tommy are caretakers at heart and watching over the shelter dogs and their neighbors was natural for them. Granite Ridge is a special place, where the love of community shines through all year. CHRISTMAS SHELTER is not only about the animals in the shelter, but about the shelter a home and community offers.

You'll want to catch up with Maddie in the next book in the series, CHRISTMAS SECRET.

Don't miss the other books in SOUL SISTERS AT CEDAR MOUNTAIN LODGE:

Book 1: Christmas Sisters –prologue book
Book 2: Christmas Kisses by Judith Keim
Book 3: Christmas Wishes by Tammy L. Grace
Book 4: Christmas Hope by Violet Howe
Book 5: Christmas Dreams by Ev Bishop
Book 6: Christmas Rings by Tess Thompson
Book 7: Christmas Surprises by Tammy L. Grace
Book 8: Christmas Yearnings by Ev Bishop
Book 9: Christmas Peace by Violet Howe
Book 10: Christmas Castles by Judith Keim
Book 11: Christmas Star by Tess Thompson
Book 12: Christmas Joy by Judith Keim
Book 13: Christmas Shelter by Tammy L. Grace
Book 14: Christmas Secret by Violet Howe
Book 15: Christmas Longings by Ev Bishop

If you enjoy Christmas stories, Tammy has written several more and invites you to read not only this series, but her other books, all featuring small towns, furry friends, and second chances.

A Season for Hope
The Magic of the Season
Christmas in Snow Valley
One Unforgettable Christmas

MORE BOOKS FROM TAMMY L. GRACE

COOPER HARRINGTON DETECTIVE NOVELS

Killer Music

Deadly Connection

Dead Wrong

Cold Killer

HOMETOWN HARBOR SERIES

Hometown Harbor: The Beginning (Prequel Novella)

Finding Home

Home Blooms

A Promise of Home

Pieces of Home

Finally Home

Forever Home

CHRISTMAS STORIES

A Season for Hope: Christmas in Silver Falls Book 1

The Magic of the Season: Christmas in Silver Falls Book 2

Christmas in Snow Valley: A Hometown Christmas Book 1

One Unforgettable Christmas: A Hometown Christmas Book 2

Christmas Wishes: Souls Sisters at Cedar Mountain Lodge

Christmas Surprises: Soul Sisters at Cedar Mountain Lodge

Christmas Shelter: Soul Sisters at Cedar Mountain Lodge

GLASS BEACH COTTAGE SERIES

Beach Haven

Moonlight Beach

Beach Dreams

WRITING AS CASEY WILSON

A Dog's Hope

A Dog's Chance

WISHING TREE SERIES

The Wishing Tree

Wish Again

Overdue Wishes

Remember to subscribe to Tammy's exclusive group of readers for your gift, only available to readers on her mailing list. **Sign up at www.tammylgrace.com. Follow this link to subscribe at https://wp.me/P9umIy-e** and you'll receive the exclusive interview she did with all the canine characters in her Hometown Harbor Series.

Follow Tammy on Facebook by liking her page. You may also follow Tammy on her pages on book retailers or at BookBub by clicking on the follow button.

FROM THE AUTHOR

Thank you for reading CHRISTMAS SHELTER. Like my readers, I've fallen in love with the characters in this series and the setting in Granite Ridge. You won't want to miss any of the SOUL SISTERS AT CEDAR MOUNTAIN LODGE BOOKS. If you're new to the series, it kicks off with a free prequel novella, CHRISTMAS SISTERS, where you'll get a chance to meet the characters during their first Christmas together.

If you enjoy women's fiction and haven't yet read my HOMETOWN HARBOR SERIES, I think you'll enjoy them. It's a six-book series, with each book focused on a different female heroine. They are set in the gorgeous San Juan Islands in the Pacific Northwest and most of the characters are a bit more seasoned. You can start the series with a free prequel that is in the form of excerpts from Sam's journal. She's the main character in the first book, FINDING HOME.

I also write my GLASS BEACH COTTAGE SERIES, set in coastal Washington and centered on Lily, a woman of fifty, who is starting her life over after losing her husband. Readers love the characters, including the furry ones in this

FROM THE AUTHOR

series, which includes BEACH HAVEN, MOONLIGHT BEACH, and BEACH DREAMS.

If you're a new reader and enjoy mysteries, I write a series that features a lovable private detective, Coop, and his faithful golden retriever, Gus. If you like whodunits that will keep you guessing until the end, you'll enjoy the COOPER HARRINGTON DETECTIVE NOVELS.

The two books I've written as Casey Wilson, A DOG'S HOPE and A DOG'S CHANCE, both have received enthusiastic support from my readers and, if you're a dog lover, are must-reads.

If you enjoy holiday stories, be sure and check out my CHRISTMAS IN SILVER FALLS SERIES and my HOMETOWN CHRISTMAS SERIES. They are small-town Christmas stories of hope, friendship, and family.

I'm also one of the founding authors of My Book Friends and invite you to join this fun group of readers and authors on Facebook. I'd love to send you my exclusive interview with the canine companions in my Hometown Harbor Series as a thank-you for joining my exclusive group of readers. You can sign up www.tammylgrace.com by clicking this link: https://wp.me/P9umIy-e

ABOUT THE AUTHOR

Tammy L. Grace is the *USA Today* bestselling and award-winning author of the Cooper Harrington Detective Novels, the bestselling Hometown Harbor Series, and the Glass Beach Cottage Series, along with several sweet Christmas stories. Tammy also writes under the pen name of Casey Wilson for Bookouture and Grand Central. You'll find Tammy online at www.tammylgrace.com where you can join her mailing list and be part of her exclusive group of readers. Connect with Tammy on Facebook at www.facebook.com/tammylgrace.books or Instagram at @authortammylgrace.

- facebook.com/tammylgrace.books
- twitter.com/TammyLGrace
- instagram.com/authortammylgrace
- bookbub.com/authors/tammy-l-grace
- goodreads.com/tammylgrace

Made in the USA
Monee, IL
16 November 2022